BLOOD ORANGES:
A Chamberlain Cotton Novel
by
H.A.L. Wagner

Published
by

FORKER MEDIA

1450 SOM Center Road, Suite 23
Mayfield Heights, OH 44024
www.forkermedia.com

BLOOD ORANGES: A CHAMBERLAIN COTTON NOVEL © 2012 H.A.L. WAGNER
ISBN: 978-0-9883972-3-1

CHAPTER
1

YESTERDAY'S high was mid-eighties. The sun was out and a blue sky pushed around balls of white fluff. In the still black of the early morning, a wet mess blew through, dropping all it had and pushing back the last of the warm air further south. I woke up on the leather sofa in my office, wrapped in nothing but the fetal position. My head wedged further down between the back and bottom cushion for warmth as hot whiskey breath reverberated back onto my face. I left the windows open, not knowing a front would push through. After all, this was Florida.

Thunder rolled through my aching head, making no distinction between the storm outside or the one in my brain, dry now after being soaked in whiskey last night. I can't seem to get to sleep without it! The sun, thankfully, kept tucked behind some grey remnants of the front. Passing car tires on the wet road below made a slashing racket that was pitch perfect to annoy the hell out of me. I slammed the two windows in my office shut. Water was draining from all sides of the building, running down gutters spilling onto sidewalks and filling into streets. I wrapped my arms around myself and shuttered.

Putting a boot to the radiator, I got it going. Damn thing hissed like a cat - but once purring left me feeling warm. I dragged myself to the closet door. Beyond the door were a set of bars. Back when my ex-partner and I were chasing bounty we had a makeshift cell put in. Made from a shark diving cage, it took up what was a closet.

I threw on a shirt and made for the toilet at the end of the hall. It was my morning routine before the other office dwellers of the second floor in this building arrived. A quick shave (on odd days) and a comb through my hair got me ready to present myself to the world. Since I couldn't remember what day it was, I skipped the shave.

Walking back, the hall was warm - warmer than my office. The maintenance men must have been watching the weather report last night. I passed several office doors with frosted glass and gold lettering ending in things like *ltd* and *Inc*. My office door just said *Private*. Most who passed through thought it was in reference to my business, a misconception I encouraged. In reality, I just never got around to pay the guys to stencil *Chamberlain Cotton Investigations*. I could probably write the expense off my taxes if I ever made enough dough to pay any.

The door marked *Private* was ajar. I never left my door open. With an open palm, I shoved it the rest of the way open and rushed in.

Henry Clementine jumped nearly three feet into the air. His narrow frame stuck the landing. "You startled me, Mr. Cotton." Henry took a seat where my head had laid minutes earlier; reminding me I needed to find a real apartment.

He took his hat off to a thinned out scalp. "Did you find anything on him?" The lean man crinkled his fedora in his hands before asking a second question. "He doesn't

[2]

know you were asking around, right?" His thin mustache danced when he spoke. Henry was near forty, with a large head on a stick frame. His suit was a well-tailored brown flannel but at least ten years old.

Still feeling the chill in my office, I kicked at the radiator once more before taking a seat in a wobbly old chair behind my desk. I pushed two empty bottles of whiskey to the edge. I reached into a bottom draw and withdrew a full bottle.

"To answer both questions: No."

"Good, that's good. I can't have Mr. Jeffers finding out I hired a private dick to follow him. Security is getting awful tight around the depot. Just yesterday I saw a man carrying a gun." Henry Clementine, the nervous client, fumbled with his tie and started to speak a few times but stopped himself. I said nothing. With a tip of the bottle, I offered a glass of sour mash. His darting eyes pulled the time from the clock on the wall. He nodded no - some men don't like to drink this early. I, however, do not like to start the day without one.

I reported to Henry all the news of tailing Clinton Jeffers, but it wasn't much. The guy had a seemingly regular life. He was out the door by eight, headed to the warehouse where he checked on his distribution company, left for a business lunch around one, and then finished his day at the courthouse. I could not report on what Jeffers was doing at the courthouse - too many cops. I am a legit detective with a license and badge, just like a dog I once had, so it wasn't that. I just do not like cops and they do not like me. Anytime the cops and I cross, it's always, "you're playing dress up" and I "need to stick to finding lost kittens" - the cute stuff.

"If there's nothing else, I'm better out on the street than behind this desk." I stood up, walked from behind the desk to the coat rack and grabbed my hat. Henry did not say anything as he made his way to the door.

"I'll let you know when I find anything Henry." I tried a smile to calm his nerves then slipped into a grey overcoat.

Out on the street, nervous guy Henry went left and I went right. I needed to go left too, but I couldn't bring myself to walk alongside him, in case his jitters where contagious. Yeah, the guy's money was green like everyone else's and that's precisely why I took the job. Henry's nervous disposition bugged the hell out of me. Nervous people were unpredictable. I had dealt with that a lot in the bounty hunting business - chumps getting squirrelly and either shooting up everything in sight or running like jackrabbits. Henry was one of those types, cowering behind an ex-girlfriend while my partner and I kick in her front door. It turned my stomach.

What was there to know about this Henry guy, anyway? I spent all this time following Jeffers, digging up the dish on him simply because a scrawny man with a nervous condition was paying me a living wage plus expenses to learn all he could about his boss. As far as I could tell, Jeffers was an all right guy running a few businesses. It was Henry with the shot nerves that roused suspicion. I stopped in my tracks, did a one eighty and double-timed it in the direction of where we had parted ways.

[4]

A chilled mist was getting heavier as I rounded the corner of Pine Street and Magnolia Avenue lowering my head to let the brim of my hat collect moisture as I moved. From above coming out of a speaker attached to a light pole, Bing Crosby carried on about it starting to look like Christmas then POP! POP! A woman screamed and tires laid rubber on the damp asphalt. Looking up, I saw the rail thin frame of a man lying half on the curb and the other half twisted in the street. The way he was sprawled out, I knew he got it from a high caliber weapon, forty at least probably a forty-five or maybe a small carbine. Nearing the body, I got a better picture. The force of the shots twisted the underweight man into an unnatural position. With his face in the gutter, his bloodied back showed the through and through.

For a moment I could not see Henry Clementine. I saw a body of a twenty-three year old woman lying in the street moments after a car accident. Her blonde hair was streaked with a sticky crimson. Her arms twisted like a Hindu god. Blood seeped from every rip in her clothing.

There was no telling how long I stood staring at the girl before I shook out the memory and knelt down going through his pockets. The cops would arrive any second leaving whatever Henry carried on him as evidence to squander. I needed to know more about what made this guy twitch.

Clutching the iron rods of a gated parking lot, another woman remained motionless, her mouth open, but no words escaped. She peeled her hands free and stood next to me.

"They just slowed down and, and then…are you a cop?" A woman appeared out of nowhere. She was tall with blond curls tucked under a hat. Her clothes were expensive, new, though now worn, and her face was heavy with makeup. First impressions, I was wishing she were prettier.

"I'm the hired kind and this guy hired me." I looked up at her from over my shoulder, "You said 'they', did you get a look at them?" I reached into Henry's upper inside coat pocket and pulled some items of various paper sizes and thickness, business cards, garage parking ticket. I didn't look, just shoved them into my own pocket.

"I kept my eyes forward, heard the shots…say, should you be rooting through his pockets. Maybe you should let-"

"Did you get a look at them or not?" I barked, then softened a bit, "How about the car?" I raised eye level with her on the curb. She backed up a few steps. Having collected all the details I could get from the barren crime scene my mind eased a bit. I stood looking at this broad taking in all she offered. On a second pass I became caught in deep, dark, eyes holding me there suspended in space. Something primal radiated from her, sending an aroma up my nose and into my brain telling me she was all woman. Wild urges began to pulsate to the beat of hide-covered drums making me forget we're supposed to be civilized.

"It was black and went that way." She pointed right and her head followed, looking down the street as if the car was still within sight. It must have been contagious because I looked as well. My stare was with purpose,

[6]

eyes searching for clues, not reliving some tragic event as she appeared to be.

"Okay, it went that way and you got no look at the driver or the shooter." I took a few steps away from the body and into the direction the woman had pointed. Screeching sirens began heading our way. Soon the place would be muddied with cops. "What's your name, lady?"

"Huh? Oh, Willimina. I have to go." Her pitch dropped. Her smooth saunter caught my eye again as her pace quickened. I liked to watch her go. I guess that is what psychologists mean by animal attraction.

I called out to her, telling her to wait for the police to take her statement. She did not care, and crossed two busy lanes of traffic to prove it. A crowd was beginning to gather. I couldn't leave Henry Clementine in the street like that to be gawked by any lookie-loos or memento seekers. The semi-circle of on-lookers was tight. A woman pushed her way to the front, only to scream and faint, forcing two business types to catch her. I noticed her eyes were open the whole time. The crowd grew thick. By the time I shoved the people back, Willimina had flagged a cab and faded out of sight, just as the black and white rolled in. The doors opened and I found myself staring down the barrel of a couple of issued 38's. I politely raised both hands.

"Okay boys you got me."

The two uniforms were young and more than likely stupid. They took my surrender a little too serious. "Hand it over grease ball!" shouted the driver of the squad car. The crowd took a step back in unison.

Get a load of this wise ass. I slowly moved with my right hand down under my coat and produced a custom model 1911 forty-five caliber. Pinching the weapon through the trigger guard, I handed it to the shorter of the two, who also happened to be the one riding shot gun, or in this case Police Standard. I knew the drill. I linked my fingers behind my head; made like I was at mass. Being a private investigator had brought more contact with the police than I would ever have liked. It came with the license, the desire to help the innocent and the overwhelming desire to punish the guilty. If I had to beat a guy to fess up, I would, and if I was exposing a grifter in his own lie, all the better. And if a thief was busted when he mistakenly robbed the police captain's house, I considered it a win.

The two uniformed officers holstered their guns. They were close enough for me to read the letters on their name tags, Polk and Connor. One beat cop stepped to the body that lay half in the street, half on the sidewalk, while the other proceeded to hassle me.

"Stupid moves rooks." I grumbled stopping the two cops in their tracks. "If I had a back up piece you both-"

The two went for their guns again, the vocal one, Polk, shouted, "Try it and you're dead." The other immediately started patting me down.

"I said 'if'. 'Tried' would mean I did and both of you would be dead. Now go check the license in my upper coat pocket and you sniff the barrel of that pistol so we can all move on to the real crime."

"Polk, check his pocket." The cop sniffed the cold steel while Polk sifted through my pockets.

"Private cop – name's Chamberlain Cotton." Polk said as he tossed the badge back at me.

"Heard of you, scab. Now what the hell happened here?" The cop handed back my piece.

"Call your lieutenant down here. Neither of you will make detective on this one." Slipping the cold steel back under my arm felt good.

The one called the other over for a powwow. Connor pulled on the radio and called out for Lieutenant Bill Blake. I recognized the southern drawl crack over the radio. The Lt. was not happy with this beat cop calling just before it was time to head home and have dinner with the wife. He shouted that it better have been for a good reason. The beat cop started with responding to a report of gunshots. The cop's slow graces were pissing me off. *Get to the point.* Polk disbursed the crowd as another black and white pulled up. More cops. It wasn't that I didn't like cops nor had respect for the law, it was that they had procedures to be followed, and I never colored inside the lines as a kid.

Lieutenant Blake arrived in a midnight blue sedan. His frame was not large but solid, you could take a sledge to him and it would bounce right off. He carried himself with importance, despite looking tired around the eyes and hungry for dinner. Blake was ten years my senior and had a bulb in his lower lip from chewing tobacco all his life. Contempt covered his face as he brushed past me without a word choosing to confer with the uniformed cops. He listened to what they had to say then looked over the body and finally came to get my story.

"Chamberlain Cotton, I thought you moved on or were dead in a gutter somewhere." Blake ran stale brown eyes over me then centered them on the body in the street, "What the hell is it this time, Cotton?" Bill said in a tiresome manner.

I lit a smoke, "His name is Henry Clementine. He had a nervous condition." Henry did not look like himself. His glasses were in the street and his skin was a pasty grey. If I had not just met with him half hour ago, I would say this was someone else.

"No wonder he was nervous, somebody shot him, twice. How'd you know him?"

"He was a client, you know, lost his cat. Did your boys in blue tell you about a gal that saw it all go down?"

Blake clinched his jaw. He shook his head no. A witness would mean questioning and questioning would lead to more suspects and he knew he would not be making it home for his wife Judy's lamb chops.

"I didn't think they had." I shifted my weight. "She's a blonde, maybe your height, with heels on of course. Told me she saw two men in a black sedan speed away after two shots rang out. I was around the corner and could hear the tires myself. The girl looked pretty shaken. I asked her a few questions but got no answers except her name - Willimina."

"I don't blame her. You ain't a cop and I don't want to stick around either. Judy's got lamb waiting for me."

"Okay Blake, play it your way and I'll play it mine." I tugged down on the brim of my hat.

"Cotton, I know you think this murder is linked to something bigger and you've probably got the scoop to prove it. So I'm gonna get this body bagged and go home to eat some chops. You're gonna kill a bottle of Walker or Daniels or any other fool with a still while hunting down Clementine's assassins." Blake did not wait for my rebuttal. He turned as the flash bulbs popped over the corpse.

Blake was right - we had done this dance before. I hated to admit it but Pine Street Pub was a block over waiting for me with a well stocked bar. This year has given me nothing but grief, and I've spent the last eight or nine months of it in a bottle. I want to come out but every time I do, the thought of her dying because I wanted to sit one out gnaws at the back of my head until it takes over every thought I have. I can't escape the memory of her death, so I'm stuck getting drunk.

Time was all I had. Lieutenant Blake had only so many men, all with other cases occupying their time. I was indeed keeping information from the Lieutenant, starting with the fact that she got into a *City Beautiful* cab versus one of the other outfits in town. This was information that would give me a jump in the case.

CHAPTER
2

I entered Pine Street Pub and it was just that - a pub, with worn wood floors and neon beer signs. The gas heater dried the air from my soggy lungs. Patrons sat smoking with sweating beers on mismatched tables and chairs, most not looking up as I passed. I made my way to a bar that stretched the rest of the wall and parked myself on a stool. Most of the city was just starting to knock-off, but, my day was just beginning. Business types began filling the joint for a snooker before they had to get home to face the wife and kids.

I looked up into the mirror and saw a familiar face that was not my own staring back at me. The hat came off as I raised a left hand to the bar keep. Knowing my order from routine the Bar Keep poured a shot of whiskey and a beer.

"How does that liver of yours still function?" the boney man in a tweed blazer on the stool next to me said, poking a finger towards my gut.

"I guess you'll find out when I'm dead - you can take it out yourself Doc." I kicked the shot back and handed the empty to the bartender. "I got another one for you by the way."

"You really keep me busy Chamberlain, you son of a bitch. Who'd you kill this time?" Doctor Keenan had the faintest of Boston accents that usually only presented itself when he was angry or drunk, which was often. His hair was the color of a rain cloud with side burns that turned darker the lower they went. Keenan was the town's coroner. For the routine stuff - old people, accidents - there were assistants. But, when there was a drug over-dose or, better yet, murder, the city got him out of bed or put on a pot of coffee and had him come down. If there is any way to be a smart drunk, it is the buddies you choose to get drunk with. The Doc was a good one for many reasons. Most importantly, Keenan controlled the knowledge; how the victim was killed and when. With knowledge came power and a tip from Doc Keenan would give me the power I needed to edge out Lieutenant Blake on a bust.

"I didn't kill anybody. My only client right now was gunned down a few blocks from here about an hour ago. Shot twice by a large caliber. A lady saw the whole thing but she split. Didn't tell her story to the cops either." I sipped the beer then waved the Bar Keeper over for another whiskey.

"Careful, not too many details, you'll ruin the surprise."

Just then the phone behind the bar rang out. The Bar Keep picked it up, nodded and looked over to Keenan. Before he could speak, Keenan spoke first, "Tell them I'm on my way." Keenan laid a five spot on bar. He put his coat on as I put my hat atop my head. We walked to the door together, stopping just before the exit. "Don't worry Chamberlain, I'll call with details." Keenan left. I stayed for another round.

The walk back to the office was cold. An Arctic wind blowing through dropped the temperature and dried the air. I took the stairs up two at a time, then down the hall to my office. Inside the office felt the same as outside - the damn radiator was out again. Thoughts of hiring some dame to answer phones and to keep up with repairs would be nice. Maybe if this town was bigger or I had more cases, I could put an ad in the paper for a secretary and base the selection on looks, but not right now. The heater would go unfixed another winter, I only used it a month or two out of the year so for now putting a shoe to it will suffice. The thing rattled and some clanking sounded somewhere along the pipe, it would be a few minutes before I would know if it was working. No matter, I was not planning to stay long.

The phone call to City Beautiful Cab Service was not as easy or fruitful as I would have liked. The bum on the other end mumbled through some Eastern European accent forcing a repeat of everything I said, something I was not accustom to doing, and when the call finally came to an end I was no closer to finding the cab then I had minutes before. I would have to just hit the streets again and hope this cabbie was still on his shift. A girl like Wilimina was not easily forgettable. Thing is, it was only a few hours after the shooting and even I was having trouble making out her face, and I had made it a point to look her dead in the eyes. It was her presence, her aura, as the Spiritualists would call it. I sat picturing her blond hair and heavy makeup. She was medium height, nothing special about her figure, except her walk, but no other real stand out qualities. Yes, the eyes... deep mocha that

[14]

seemed endless - the kind of orbs that looked right through a guy. Her alluring eyes made me wish the rest of her had more to offer.

Back on the damp streets, I found myself humming a Christmas tune I had heard earlier that day while the sun was still in the sky. Now in the dark it was all the more difficult to spot the numbers on the cabs as they passed by. I waved down the random few cabs left on the street, looked for the right company then the right number. No luck. It was getting late and I already had stopped in at more than a few bars to get a shot of warmth in my bones. I found in the past, stopping in for a drink gifted more information than beating a dirty street. The last place I stopped was *Taps*.

Taps was the watering hole you would expect it to be - a regular shrine for all those that fell in the line of duty, whether it was in war or on the beat on the hard knock streets of this or any other dirty city. The inside was long and narrow. The bar ran along the left wall with tables on the right. An open area in the back sat a pool table. The walls were covered in pictures of cops, firemen and servicemen overseas. This was the joint of last resort for me. There was the good and the bad of the place. Starting with the bad, it was always filled with cops or ex-cops. The good part was that a place like Taps could erupt into a brawl. Of course, with everyone being some kind of civil servant, the law was ironically never involved. If I kept my head low and my face in an empty mug, then no one would bother me. Too bad I was here for information.

Andy, the bar keep, was missing his right arm. The bottom of his sleeve was pinned to the top. His jaw was covered in copper hair with exposed flesh where a mustache would hang. Andy was an all right guy in my book. For a while now I could rely on Andy for accurate information. I would throw questions his way, usually with a C note for a tip, and the information always panned out. There was one thing that really irked me about Andy, and that was the story of his missing arm. The one-armed barkeep spoke the truth about everything but the story of his missing arm. Over the years, I had heard many stories. Most of the time it was the usual drunks coming around, gathering a few more drunks together and the inevitable question would slur from their lips…*Where'd you lose the arm?*

The bar keep was good natured about it. His stories would vary. Once it was in Hong Kong while serving as a Merchant Marine. Another time, it was rescuing a child from a burning orphanage back in his firefighter days. It was clear from the photos of Andy over the bar he had done all things he claimed to, but I had to assume it was from doing something stupid. Hell, we all do stupid things every day on the job. Just running into oncoming gunfire or a burning building was stupid. But to lose an arm must have been real stupid. Either way, it worked out for the one-armed bar keep. He somehow managed to land a fine looking Irish bride. Nadine was 5'2" and full of spit and fire but she kept the real rowdiness down so a guy could have a quiet drink. She also kept the bar stocked with the finest Irish whiskeys to ever cross my lips.

"Andy." I called the bar keep over.

"Hi, aw Cotton. What'll it be?"

"No I'm fine for now. I got a question for you." I licked my lips. They were dry and starting to crack.

"Good cause I owe my bookie a few dollars. What is it?" Andy leaned in towards me to keep Nadine from over-hearing the conversation. She kept tight rules and Taps was no speak-easy. The problem with Andy was there was no whisper. He had one volume setting and that was loud.

"I saw a girl get into a City Beautiful cab today and I'm trying to track it down, see where it dropped her."

"Oh I get it, a real looker huh?" Andy licked his lips; Nadine was proof enough he had a thing for the pretty gals. Who doesn't? But Nadine could hear a mouse fart from across the room. She looked over with icicles in her eyes, and then began collecting glasses working her way towards the two of us.

"Something like that. It was cab number twenty six."

"We got a couple a regular cabbies in here. I don't know if they're finishing their shift or just starting it. Did you get a look at the driver?" Andy poured me a beer out of habit.

"This guy was wearing a cap, but this time of year who ain't? I'm guessing he was thin. I recall a pencil neck poking through the top of his collar."

"Reggie!" Nadine shouted, now only a few feet from the two of us. "It's probably Reggie that swine bastard." Nadine kept the troublemakers out but she was not beyond causing it herself.

"You sure about that sunshine?"

"Like the sunshine ore me arse. He's a slime ball, that one. Gave him the boot not too long ago. Caught 'em

[17]

trying to take advantage of a lady who's had too much for the night, he was. I saw in his eyes what he had planned." She shoved the empties across the bar to Andy.

Good, a real sleaze. That always makes it more fun while twisting arms.

"Easy now, Nadine. We can't throw out every Joe who comes in trying to pick up a lady." Andy stood erect now that there was no point in whispering.

"Aw, trash he is. Usually comes in and sits in the corner waiting for gals to have their limit and then offers them a ride in his cab. That's his game."

"Fine, fine, how about I just take his usual seat for tonight?" I took my beer and walked back to the poorly lit corner booth.

"Alright Cotton, but you take trouble out the back door, hear?" Nadine headed back to whatever chore had occupied her before she budded in. I did not bother with a reply. I was waiting for my prey, a dirtball cabbie taking advantage of girls who didn't know their limits. A broken right arm ought to be enough to get the guy to talk and keep him from driving for a few weeks. I could already hear the bone snap as the cabbie cried out with an address for this Wilimina.

The cabbie was late to the show and as such the suds kept coming, I was burning through what little profits Clementine had afforded me. With him taking two in the chest, there would be no more paydays. If I were smart, I would let it be and free my time for a paying gig. In my beer-filled gut, I knew Jeffers had something to do with Clementine's death. Powerful men like him enjoy their risks. Taking out my bread and butter was a risk beyond managing for Jeffers.

I made my way to the bar for a cup of Joe to straighten out my eyesight. As I turned with a cup of steaming Columbian, a man with a pencil neck and familiar cap came through the door of Taps. He headed straight for the dark corner, his usual spot. I leaned against the bar and studied the gawky cab driver. His hair was shaggy and tucked mostly under his paperboy cap. His coat was a fresh cut style but already dirty. It wasn't his, leading me to believe it was left behind by some businessman who had the miss fortune of taking a ride in his cab. He had close-set eyes and a big nose, probably broken more than once. *So he can tolerate some pain. This should go well.*

The cabbie took his seat in the dim lit corner. From that back booth he could see the whole place, war trophies and all. I leaned with the bar to my mid-back and watched the cabbie for a moment or two, then looked away. This went on for an hour as Andy brought the man a few rounds. Then a girl stumbled in. The cabbie perked up as he watched her turn down what was probably a couple of retired cops as she made her way over to me. I made the mistake of looking her way.

"Hey Andy." The red head slurred, never taking her green eyes from mine. "Can I get a seven and seven?" She leaned into me. Her breath smelled like the bottom of a garbage can. She's probably already puked once tonight, enough to keep her on her feet. I whispered something in her ear that made her draw back then giggle and lose interest. She took her fizzing drink and staggered over to the cabbie.

[19]

The two seemed to hit it off and soon the cabbie ordered another round for the lady. "This time make it a double." He said as his wormy hands slipped around the red head's waist. This went on for a couple of more rounds, then, as the girl began to blink in and out of consciousness, the cabbie decided it was time to be a good Samaritan and take her home, or to a back alley. "Someone here call a cab?" he joked as he helped her to the door. Most of the other drunks were gone or caught up in their own self-importance to notice the cabbie drag the woman out, except me. Once the door closed after them, I waited a few moments for a buffer before I started my tail.

Outside, the city's tropical latitude took the bite out of the Arctic air funneling through the buildings along the street below, but it was still cold. I kept my head tilted down to keep my hat from flying off against the gusts. Looking down Orange Avenue, two red taillights came on, catching my attention. I quickened my pace to my own heap. Finding out the cabbie was a creep meant he would not talk easy or cheap. There would have to be physical persuasion to get what I wanted. The objective would be to catch the guy when he was most vulnerable, with his pants down.

The cab moved from its spot and cut down a side street. I fired the Red Diamond motor in my International KB pickup and pulled out after them. As he led me through empty downtown streets, I had a good idea where he was taking the girl - it would be over the tracks, then down to an empty lot. A single thirty-foot tall concrete block wall stood in front of what was a furniture warehouse. Parked alongside it, no one could see you from the road. I knew the spot alright - it was great for taking someone when you didn't want to be bothered.

I cut the lights then killed the engine, coasting the binder along the curb of Concord Street. I couldn't wait too long. This guy might be quick - maybe that's why he needs them drunk. It cuts down on the insults if they're passed out. I got out of my car and into the cold night. I shoved my hands into warm coat pockets as I made my way to the cab. I could hear the commotion before I ever saw the car.

The cab sat parked next to the wall. The dome light was on inside and heated breath fogged the windows. I rapped on the glass of the side window. The gawky man smeared a hand over the fogged window and pressed his face against the cold glass to catch an eye of who it was. I dropped the butt of my pistol against the window shattering it. The cab driver cried out and the girl beneath him moaned through her stooper. I reached in and unlocked the rear passenger door and grabbed hold of the bleeding man, dragging him onto the broken concrete.

Reggie got up quickly with one hand on his splintered face and the other in the air. Then Reggie said, "Take the money and the girl if you want her."

"I don't want either. I want information."

"I ain't got nothing for you."

"Sure you do, bud." I used my left hand to grab Reggie's out-stretched arm, pulling him near, then I tossed a right back at him. Reggie stumbled back but did not go down. A few more punches were thrown. I batted him around like a cat with a mouse, just toying with him. I wasn't going to let it get heavy unless Reggie wanted it that way.

"Okay what do you want to know?" Reggie spat a wad of saliva and blood. The girl attempted to sit up in the back seat of the cab. Still blitzed out of her mind, she slipped back into unconsciousness.

"You picked up a blond today."

"She was more of a strawberry blond, but I ain't got preferences." Reggie could take a beating and I wanted desperately to give him one. Slime like this needed to be disposed of. Sure, the broad in the back seat got herself in this jam by refusing to put the bottle down, but girls like her didn't need vultures like Reggie circling.

"Sarcasm will get you dead. Shut your mouth until I'm done asking the question or I'll break your damn skull in half." I snarled. In the dim frozen night, Reggie could see a glint of teeth, knowing I would make good on my promise.

"Okay chum. Just where did I pick her up?"

"Magnolia and Pine Street, about five. She was in a hurry to get out of there."

"Oh yeah, she told me to just drive fast for a few blocks. Crazy lady, pretty shaken up by... were you after her?" Reggie moved toward his cab. He turned his back to me. I let my attention slip to the red head in his back seat. The girl, with eyes closed, grabbed at the hem of her raised skirt trying to pull it over her knees for warmth.

"Hey bud, I'm asking the questions. Where did you drop her?"

Reggie got closer to the opened passenger side door. "Aww, not sure... let me think." In one motion, Reggie dove in and reached under the seat pulling up a .38. As he spun, his right arm raised to shoot. I pounced. My right arm tucked under Reggie's, and then hooked my palm over the back of Reggie's neck. I raised my right knee and drove it into the cab driver's chest with such force it expelled all the air in the man's lungs and cracked his sternum. The pistol dropped to the ground. Reggie lay there attempting to breath. He struggled for several seconds as I stood over him.

"Where did you drop her?" Steam ventilated from my open mouth.

"Robinson and Primrose." Reggie said through wheezing gasps for air. "I watched her get into a pearl colored sedan. You're gonna want to know this; she took off the blond wig she was wearing. I don't care for brunettes." Reggie cracked a broken smile as shards of glass pushed to the skin's surface.

I tossed the .38 into the dark night. I reached into the back seat and scooped out the red head. She groaned a little at first then buried her head into my shoulder. *Stupid girl. I won't be here next time.*

The girl was a waste of my time but somewhere someone had to cut her a break. Hoping the address on her id was current, I drove a couple miles out of my way to drop her. Third floor apartment with no lift, last door on the left and I had to carry the dame all the way. I dug out her keys in the clutch, opened the door and tossed her on the couch, propping her on her side in case she vomited.

I stood over the helpless girl. I began to break apart what went wrong in her life that would cause her to get drunk with a cabbie and let him take her for a ride. It was a wasted thought and I waved it off. It didn't matter, the damage was done.

***

The night air dipped, the coldest point in the night was still a few hours away. I wanted to be home, or at least on my office couch, with a wool blanket thrown over me for when it hit. My nose was red and beginning to drip as I made my way east on Colonial Drive to my truck. It was getting so late that soon it would be getting early.

A long black sedan of well-being pulled along the grimy curb, smearing the white walls of the passenger side tires with gutter muck. The rear door opened and a black pistol with a barrel circumference big enough for me to stick my finger in pointed out. A twitch of the gun told me what to do and so I climbed into the car. Immediately the tires spun and the car lurched forward. I grabbed at a hanging strap just above the window.

Passing street lamps provided a second's description of my new company. To my left was a man with similar proportions as myself. Opposite me sat an elderly man but still full of testosterone. In his grey overcoat, with a dyed grey fur collar nearly the same color as his own hair, I guessed he was giving the orders. He had gloved hands that clenched a cane. In a flash of a street lamp I recognized him as the man I was hired to tail. Mr. Clinton Jeffers studied me before saying a word.

"So you are the Private Cop." Jeffers finally said. I placed his accent as New England, Vermont probably.

"Yep."

[24]

All three of us sat in silence. The car made its third right hand turn. We were just going around in circles so I relaxed.

"You kill Clementine?" I tossed that out as I reached for a smoke with my left hand. The Gunman shoved the piece into my shoulder reminding me I shouldn't get too relaxed.

Jeffers said nothing. He dropped his left hand down and popped open a small compartment containing cigarettes. He picked one and handed it to me. I took it, shoving it in between my lips and let it dangle there waiting for a light. The flame came from the gunman. He flipped the Zippo back, allowed me a few puffs then dropped it back into his pocket. I turned to the gunman.

"You kill Clementine?" I asked making reference to the hand cannon poking my side.

Jeffers answered for him, "No, not him nor I Mr. Cotton. Did you kill Henry, Mr. Cotton?" The rich old man dragged on a cigarette, turning his head slightly to the left as he exhaled.

Was this guy for real? I shifted in my seat. "And lose my only meal ticket at the moment, nuts to that."

"Good to hear Mr. Cotton and there may be another meal ticket here if you are interested." Another drag and another head turn to exhale. This guy was irritating me.

"You want me to snoop around for you, is that it? What if you don't like what I find? You going to put two in my chest like Clementine?" I did not like where this was going. Getting further into this murder was what I wanted, but not at the control of Jeffers. I've seen this before - I get hired to prove Jeffers did not kill Henry while all the time some innocent sap gets the blame. That sap could be anyone, the gunman to my left or even me.

"You've already done your snooping around me and my man Careep here, and you came up with nothing. I, however, started my own investigation on you the first day you tailed my car. Very interesting life you have lived Mr. Cotton. It was a shame letting a woman come between you and your former partner, quite a messy falling out you had." Jeffers petted a folder that had been next to him on the seat.

"That was a long time ago, bud." The past was dead and sorted for me. "My business is my own and I wouldn't say I've come up with nothing. Now are you going to tell me what or who you want me to look into or are we going to reminisce about the old days?"

"In time. First, let us get to know one another. Despite your past incapabilities, the mere fact you are still alive tells me you are competent at your job. Henry was not completely foolish in his suspicions of me and my operations. You see Mr. Cotton, I am a man of power and influence here in our little community. I have abused that power." The car made another right turn. Jumping out of a moving car was an option I had exercised before. I sized up Careep once more and decided against it. Jeffers continued, "I want to know what you dug up for Henry."

"You eat a lot of tuna." I shot him a grin; I had enough of this stand off. Being questioned was not one of my strong suits.

Jeffers waved a hand and somehow through the dark, the driver caught sight of it. The car pulled along the curb and stopped. Jeffers leaned forward stacking one hand on top of the other over the cane handle. "It's getting late. At some point Mr. Cotton, you will need to play ball with me." He reached out and grabbed the door handle.

Careep gave me a shove sliding me off my seat and crashing into the gutter. My elbow hit the concrete, the damp cold magnifying the pain. The window on the car rolled down. Jeffers stuck his wrinkled face out into the cold.

"I pay very well Mr. Cotton. Do reconsider."

The car sped away blowing hot exhaust in my face. I was slow getting to my feet. It was almost five now and I needed to get some sleep. In a few hours, Lieutenant Blake would be calling with questions I could not answer.

CHAPTER
3

BACK in my office the only heat was a bulb I left burning at my desk. I wrapped myself in a grey wool blanket I had in the closet and laid out on the couch. The ash tray was on my chest as I smoked what was left of my pack. A hundred random pieces of evidence floated in my blank head like planets in the emptiness of space. Each one could be related or totally separate, with nothing necessarily connecting them. Clementine took two bullets because he was suspicious of Jeffers. A painted up blonde who was not a blonde witnessed the whole thing and took off with out a statement to police. Jeffers knew he was in it enough to have an armed guard. That is where I will have to start in the morning. I snubbed out my last smoke and rolled into the couch.

The phone was ringing, but in the blackness of my mind, I refused to accept it. By the time I rubbed my eyes open, the ringing stopped. The possibility it was all a dream lingered until it started all over again. I jerked the cord out of the wall and the phone went back to sleep as I did.

It felt like five minutes later when the knocking started. The blanket was on the floor and I was balled up with my face in the cushion.

"Cotton, open up." It was Lieutenant Blake.

My throat was dry, air passed my vocal cords sending out a cat licking sandpaper. I cleared my throat and tried again.

"Coming." I managed to get out.

"Chocolate chips, Cotton. Hurry it up." Blake never liked to swear so he substituted cuss words with other words. This method was effective for him and entertained the rest of us.

I flipped the lock and he twisted the knob. I took a seat at my desk and splashed some bourbon in a glass. Blake had not shaved and his tie was tight against his neck. He was out late on this Clementine case.

"Chocolate chips, what happened to you, you son of a baker?"

I sucked back the whiskey and it cleared my throat.

Blake shook his head disapprovingly at the empty bottles of whiskey and beer before sitting on my couch. He pushed up the brim of his hat and let out a heavy breath. "Already drinking Cotton?"

"Mouth wash, but you didn't come here for an intervention. What'd Doc find out about Henry?"

Blake grumbled. He was not one for answering questions either. "Because he was your client, I'll let you in on what I have. Nobody saw anything. One person told an officer that she saw a blond lady headed the opposite direction as they all flooded to the scene. So that backs up what you said."

We sat staring at each other. He tongued at the empty tobacco socket in his lower lip while his patience slipped away. Four round stubby fingers dug into a wool pant leg.

Blake exhaled exaggeratedly, "Jumping butter balls, Cotton! Have you got anything or don't you?"

With a smile letting him know I cracked him, I said, "Nope."

Blake rolled out of the couch, rising to his feet. He started for the door, cut back a few steps and paused.

"Cotton, go take a leap." He stabbed a finger at me then waved me off, "Oh never mind. You make sure and call me when you get something, just so you don't get accidentally shot by one of my men." He left the door open when he exited.

I always got push-back for being honest. I closed the door and circled my sparse office. Jeffers had given Blake nothing to go on either. Splitting the blinds, I looked at the street below. Low clouds made everything grey, making it impossible to tell what time it was. People moved about in lighter jackets and less over coats. The front was pushing through. Today's temperature would be ten degrees warmer.

I looked at my watch. Jeffers would be fast into his daily routine overseeing activities at the loading docks. That is where I would start my day.

Getting out of downtown was a slow go. Christmas shoppers were beginning to fill the streets, carrying arms full of wrapped gifts, forcing a wide birth. Cars circled blocks looking for the best parking spot. As I pulled away from the curb the fight for my spot sounded with a couple of horns blowing.

I headed south for a few miles until buildings and houses gave way to orange groves. I turned down a limestone road. The previous day's rain kept the dust

[30]

down, and it was a good thing because I was sandwiched in a string of heavy-duty trucks with empty beds, making their way to the depot. I burned the clutch as the line stopped and started - there was no way to see the end. I dropped the shifter down a gear and gunned the motor, swinging the wheel to the right. The inline six worked overtime to turn the gears as the tires dug deep into the soup along the road. Traction was tough to come by as limestone mixed with decomposing plant life forming grey primordial ooze. I was glad to have put tractor tires in the rear last year. They made a racket on-road but couldn't get any better off-road.

Finally, the narrow road opened into a large distribution warehouse covering five acres of covered building, easily. A large white oval sign, ringed in blue, then red hung above the depot, declaring in fanciful script: this was indeed *Jeffers's Distribution Depot*. On one side of the depot, trucks backed into loading docks, butting up against four-foot high concrete walls to get to ground level with the dock. On the other side of the warehouse sat train tracks. A horn blew repeatedly as an engine rolled in with a line of cars I could not see the end of. I splashed through rain-filled potholes and parked on the highest ground available.

The air was heavy with carbon exhaust as I neared the depot on foot. Trucks passed by, coming and going. Engines rattled to get out of their own way as gravel crunched under heavily loaded trucks. I spotted Jeffers's long black sedan, the one he so wonderfully toured me around the city in. The driver sat behind the wheel with a cigarette between his fingers and an open newspaper spread out before him. We made eye contact for several seconds. He nearly dropped the cigarette in his lap setting off the newspaper as he scrambled out of the car. The driver was quick on his feet to cut me off at the stairs leading up to the dock.

"Hey Mac, does the boss know your coming?"

"Your crotch is smoking."

He looked down and I shoved him out of my way. I was up the steps before he could get up out of the dirt. The scuffle caught some unwanted attention as the dock foreman quickly stepped in.

"Can I help you mister?" He said, taking off thick leather gloves. The foreman was tall and lean with a hard living face, making it impossible to place his age.

"I'm here to see Jeffers." I said, glancing back to see the driver wiping yellow-grey limestone off his black suit.

"You got a delivery or sumptin'?" he asked. I shook my head no. "Well then it ain't my department. Go on inside and up the latter to the offices. You'll find him in there." He pointed back into the dark recesses of the warehouse. I nodded my reply and made my way in.

The floor of the warehouse was bustling with conveyor belts, pushing oranges and grapefruits, as men in overalls and leather gloves shoveled fruit into crates stamped with an array of chain markets from Florida and beyond. I dodged a few workers in tractors hauling a train of crated produce, yelling at me to get out of their way. I fully believe they had no intentions of stopping. The sound of tape ripping off the soles of my shoes came with each step as I made my way across the sticky floor to the ladder. The steps up the office were steep and narrow. The metal frame wobbled and pinged once or twice before I made it to the top. A row of offices with large bay windows lined the south wall of the warehouse. A gangplank ran the length in front. Passing the nearest window, I saw the first women of the day. Four rows thick of girls punching at typewriters and flipping through inventory lists. On to the next window I found a few interior offices. I let myself in.

Closing the door behind me relieved my ears of the racket from below. At the front desk was a secretary with tight wound black hair. She wore horn-rimmed glasses and bit her nails. Her face was round and sagged below the jaw line. She was tearing at a hanging nail when she saw me.

"Yes, can I help you?" She said spitting out the tiny nail remnant.

"Mr. Jeffers, please." I pulled my hat off my head and held it with two hands.

"Oh he isn't here." She forced a smile to ease the dullness of her face.

"I met his driver outside so I -"

"Well what I mean to say is he isn't in *this* office. Go two doors down. You should find him there." She dipped her head and went right back into her work.

I saw myself out. Back on the gangplank, noise from the warehouse floor echoed up into the steel rafters. I counted two doors and made my way in.

The room was quiet, except for the tick and tock of a clock. The carpet was a dark brown and the walls, wood-paneled. A pair of mountain landscape portraits hung on the walls to either side of me. Directly ahead of me sat a large deep cherry wood desk. Behind it, leaning back in a leather bound swivel chair sat Careep. In the light of the desk lamp, I could make out features undefinable from the dark early morning ride. His complexion was that of old paper. His eyes were large and round redwood orbs, focusing in on me. His rolled up shirtsleeves exposed coarse black hair on his forearms, matching the hair on his scalp. The pen in his right hand was set down as he moved the hand over an opened top drawer.

"There's no need for that, Careep." I stood in the middle of the room.

Careep remained quiet as he grabbed the receiver with his other hand, leaving nothing to chance. He mumbled something and waited for a reply, then hung up.

A buzzer unlocked the office door behind Careep. He never took his eyes off me as I moved past him.

Clinton Jeffers's office was the same size as my own. I thought with all this square footage he would spring for something better, but it was an indication of the kind of frugal businessman he was. The wood paneling continued along his office walls. Gold-framed diplomas and certificates dotted the walls, a few of them photos with elected officials. His desk was a thing of art. It was carved wood resembling detail you would find in a gothic cathedral. Up top, it was neatly organized with two phones and penholder. Two folders, one green the other red, lay on opposite sides.

"Usually powerful men pick pretty ladies to be their secretaries." I said taking a seat in one of two plush chairs in front of the desk.

"Women can be persuaded by tall good looking men, such as yourself, to do things I might not like. Careep

[34]

cannot." The old man was sharp and I liked his logic. Maybe if I ever do get that assistant, I'll pick off a list of mugs rejected from the police academy. Behind him was a tray full of gold, brown and clear liquors. Suddenly my mouth was dry I needed to wet it. My palms became moist; I wiped them on my pant legs. It was a bad tell on my part. Jeffers caught my eyes and swiveled in his chair forty-five degrees. He asked if it was too early for a drink. I waved it off, but felt inside I could use one.

"The way Lieutenant Blake broke up the best night's sleep I've had in months, I'm guessing he stopped by and you gave him nothing."

Jeffers opened a pewter box and pulled a cigar. Without saying he offered me one. I took him up on it and waited for the lighter. We sat puffing, twisting the cigars between our sealed lips. The smoke floated between us, catching in the light and streaking silver and white across the room.

"Mr. Cotton I told him what he needed to know. Henry, God rest him, was an employee of mine. I showed Lieutenant Blake the folder we had on him. I explained that I was unaware of any dealings of Henry's that might have contributed to his death. I was hoping you would have information for me." He puffed once more then set the cigar in the ashtray. His eyes had not changed since I walked through the door. His stare was solid without being pushy, and no matter what I said, his expression would not change. He was a guy holding all the cards.

"Everyone is into sharing these days. Okay, here it goes. You're dirty Jeffers. Somehow, someway, you're dirty and Henry was on to that. He was a scared, frail man that probably would just as easily been scared to death than be shot. I want Henry's employee file and access to what he was working on for the last three months."

"Lieutenant Blake is getting a warrant for that information as we speak. Corporate secrets you know." He leaned back in his double stuffed black leather chair blowing smoke around the room.

"I don't need a warrant." I stood up and leaned over his desk just an arm's grab away from him. I jabbed out the cigar into the tray.

"By all means Mr. Cotton." Jeffers's eyes turned into slits. He reached into a drawer somewhere deep in the massive desk and pulled a brown folder and a large leather bound ledger. The folder was about an inch thick stuffed with papers, the ledger at least two inches thick. His hand shook slightly as he handed it over. I didn't know if it was his age or I was getting to him.

Jeffers continued, "I believe you to be as good as you believe you are, Cotton. I could use you on my side. Whatever your daily rate is I will double it."

I took the folder saying, "You may have deep ties and a far reach in this town, but I won't let you pull my strings." I made for the door. I could hear his chair push back as Jeffers got to his feet. He slammed down on his desk. A buzz sounded just before the door opened. Careep stood filling the jam. His size was another detail I missed in the dark.

Careep puffed his chest and I took a step back to plant my feet. Careep thought I was making a move upstairs so he held up his arms. I donkey kicked him hard in the knee and he folded. I pushed his out-swung arm inwards and stepped behind him. Giving him a firm shove, he dove into one of the chairs, breaking it against the weight of the ornately carved desk.

"I'll make you a deal, Clinton. If the trail doesn't lead back to you or your boy here you can pay me double my daily rate." I closed the door on my way out.

I pulled out of the yard in a hurry and drove a few miles jetting up and down random streets, cutting a path back towards town. If Jeffers had sent Careep out after me it was too late. I pulled over to a corner market off Michigan Avenue. I bought a paper and a juice. Sitting in my truck, I went over Henry's file. The sun was out now. Its warming rays absorbed into the black leather seat, radiating heat through the cab.

Yellow carbon copies of above-satisfactory reviews every quarter for the last eight years populated the folder. His official title was Route Manager. I leafed through the ledger. It was a log of truck numbers coming and going - when they arrived, departed, what route they took and when they got to the designated destination. He also kept the service logs for all of Jeffers' trucks. An insurance form listed an unwed sister in Indiana. Since Henry listed Indiana as his home address, nothing seemed odd about it. Just to be safe, I jotted her name and number down on a notepad. Sifting through the file, I hoped something would jump out at me - nothing did. Henry was an efficient and reliable employee. There were no disciplinary write-ups of any kind. Most bosses could not ask for more.

I scanned the newspaper. The article on Henry was short - just that a man was shot on the three hundred block of Magnolia and some witnesses were questioned. I liked the line about several leads, the cops did not have a clue or, if they did, they were not sharing with the press. I went back through the employee file. There had to be something I missed.

Ten minutes later, I sat with half a bottle of cranberry juice and papers scattered over the cab of my pickup. My eyes lazily gazed out over the wheel and onto the traffic coming and going down Michigan Ave. A truck marked with the Jeffers logo passed by under load weighted down with produce headed for any number of area grocers, or beyond. I fired up the International and drove on back to my office.

CHAPTER
4

I had my sport coat slung over one shoulder and my hat pushed back high on my head as I made my way down the over-heated hallway toward my office. Seated on a narrow bench near a water fountain was a pair of legs that disappeared into a purple woven dress. A wide black belt was synched tight around her slender waste. Dark chestnut curls brushed the tops of her shoulders that tucked up under her purple hat, topped with a felt flower. She looked me in the eye, then down to the floor, wiping her hands on her dress. She must be here for me.

The key loosened the lock on my door and I stood to the side with it open. Her eyebrows pushed together as she sorted it out, then got up and preceded me inside.

"Have a seat. Would you like a drink?" I had my back to her as I poured some whiskey into a glass. She was silent, so I looked over my shoulder, holding up the bottle. She nodded yes and I poured a second glass. She took it and gulped it down.

"Nervous?" I asked leaning half on my desk, one leg dangling above the floor.

"Yes, I suppose." Her voice was soft with an innocence of never having been in a private detective's office before. She stood looking around at the empties littered in my office before taking a seat on the couch.

"Henry was your brother." I stated for her.

"Why yes, he was." Rose color filled her cheeks. The liquor was warming her from the inside. She cleared her throat, and this time the innocence was repressed, "I'm here with regards to his insurance."

"I don't really handle that sort of thing. Henry hired me to look into something for him but as far as insurance and wills and such, it's out of my hands." I poured a second round for the both of us. I think I liked this bolder sister over the softer one.

"Mr. Jeffers has already helped me on that end. I was there to see him today and he wrote me out a personal check and said he would deal with the claim instead of making me wait." This time she sipped the whiskey. She reached into her handbag and produced a signed personal check from Clinton Jeffers to Ms. Sonya Clementine for twenty-five thousand dollars. I fought to keep my face frozen.

"I want to hire you to finish what Henry started."

My face shriveled and sucked in at her request. Working for dames was the worst. Women always expected more out of you then men do. They all think I can leap tall buildings in a single bound because I have a P.I.'s badge.

Her soft doe eyes began to tear up. She pulled a handkerchief and blotted them at the corners. Aw hell, I owe it to her brother.

"Okay Ms. Clementine, what can I do for you?" I took a seat behind my desk.

"Henry phoned me two days ago and said he was on to something at work, something about random accidents that were not random at all. I told him he was just being silly and needed to take a few days off. I told him I would come down and meet him at the beach for a rest. He agreed, and when I checked into the hotel there was an urgent message waiting for me." She fought the tears back. I could see she had been at it a while now and her ducts did not have much left. She was a well put together Midwestern girl. She had manners and posture with an enduring spirit that made her determined to flourish in any environment and right now, it was the toughest of environments.

I opened the employee file on Henry. She continued speaking. "The police were the ones that lead me to you, Mr. Cotton." She blotted each eye before putting the handkerchief away.

I could see Henry around her eyes and a little in the high cheekbones, but I was not totally convinced. It may be something I wanted to believe.

"Did Henry say why he hired me – I mean, specifically say?" I finished the whiskey and lit a cigarette.

Sonya blinked a few times, but otherwise was still. She said, "Well, he wanted to be sure of some suspicions. I don't really know what. He was pretty rattled, whatever it was."

"Are you staying in town tonight, Ms. Clementine, or going back to the beach?"

"Sonya… please, call me Sonya, and yes I've booked a room at the Orange Court Hotel."

I sat, letting my cigarette burn down, staring at her. She became uncomfortable with the glare, shifting in her seat, her legs pinned at the knees, tacked like a sail in shifting winds.

"Were you close to your brother?" I asked taking a final drag of the cigarette before smashing it out.

"As close as siblings ten years apart can be I suppose." She kept her face a blank stare, what little emotion she had left was firmly repressed.

"I have the books and logs he kept at the office, tracking shipments and such. Could you take a look? You might catch something I didn't." I stood up, collected the paperwork from my desk and walked it over to her on the couch. I sat beside her and she shot me a crooked grin. Without realizing it, I inhaled deep, taking in a fresh scent of lavender and vanilla. It was a clean smell, the other end of the spectrum of usual stale smoke and dried rum I was used too.

Sonya's brow came together as her red painted nail scrolled along the log lines in the book. She repeated dragging her finger down a second time, then stopped. As she scanned the ledger I found myself locked on to her every move.

"I'm sorry Mr. Cotton, I just don't see anything out of the ordinary." She closed the book and handed it to me.

"I was just about to go to your brother's apartment. Do you feel up to it?" I stood up and grabbed my sport coat.

Sonya got to her feet and finished the last of the whiskey in her glass. "I would like that Mr. Cotton." She put the glass down and smoothed out her dress with both hands.

"Cotton, just call me Cotton." I smiled.

We hopped in the pickup and bounced a few blocks, down brick-laden and oak-lined streets. The road ended at a lake, half a mile wide. We went left, following the lake halfway around. The houses gradually grew in size along with the cars parked in front of them. The lawns were deep with wrap-around driveways and large arches marking the entrance. Much of the architecture highlighted Spanish styling, large white plaster walls capped with burnt red terracotta roof tiles.

"Wow, are we headed in the right direction to my brother's place?" Sonya soaked up the local Florida style.

"Yep, just about there." I cut a left again, heading away from the lake. A block down on the right, we parked along the street.

The house was a brown English Tutor, out of the norm for this block. A sloping pitched roof covered the large red door. Two green cone-shaped pines flanked each side of the porch. We walked up the drive, passing the front of the house. Sonya questioned with out saying a word and I pointed to the garage in the back. Over it was a small apartment.

A flight of wooden stairs, badly in need of repainting, led us to a screen door. It screeched loudly as I pulled it back. Sonya held it open as I slid my pocketknife blade between the bolt and the jam. I gave the handle a jiggle and the door opened.

Inside the small studio, a bed filled the corner, with a dresser at the foot and a desk in the other corner. In the back were two doors, one led to a kitchen and the other to a bathroom. I did not know if Henry was the tidy sort or a slob. The place look organized but certainly rifled through. My guess it was the cops because nothing appeared broken or over turned.

Sonya stared saucer-eyed at a photo of her, Henry and their mother. In the picture, Sonya was sitting on the hood of a Buick while Henry had his arm around their mother. She cradled the photo.

"His first new car..." She whispered only half intending for me to hear. I looked over as we made eye contact. She spoke up, "He bought it when he got his first job. That was back in Indiana. It was another few years before he came to Florida to work for Jeffers."

"Cute kid." I said pointing at the girl in the photo.

Sonya held it out in front of eyes filled with memories. "I guess I was about twelve." She put the picture down softly on the desk. She turned to me while I sifted through a dresser drawer.

"We need something that will shed light on what Henry found out about Clinton Jeffers, or someone he was dealing with." I glanced over at her. Her eyes were black narrow slits as hatred for her brother's murderer boiled behind them. I suddenly became aware I was digging through a dead man's belongings. I tried to put the clothes in the drawer back in a folded position.

"Why bother straightening? It's not like he is coming back." Venom coated her words as she balled her fists.

"Look I'm sorry but -"

She lunged towards me with flailing arms. I caught one at the wrist, the other bounced off my chest. I held her tight so she could not hurt either of us. She squirmed, mumbled, and spat.

"Hey, hey it wasn't me, remember? I want the bastards that did it, same as you." I got her in a bear hug and she went limp. We walked together over to the bed and sat down. Both her arms pulled tight and folder up over her chest. I rubbed the upper part of her arms.

I spoke softly, "When you were kids, was there a place that Henry would hide anything he wanted kept secret?"

She frowned and shook her head no. I stood up and headed back to the dresser. There was no time to play nursemaid to the kid sister. She needed to toughen up quick or head back to Indiana. I was pulling out the second drawer when she said, "He hid a burlesque show flyer under his bed for years between the box and mattress."

Together, we pulled the mattress up. There, in a manila envelope was another ledger. I uttered something about being a good sister and snatched up the book.

We sat on the couch flipping through it. The pages were the same as the original.

"I don't get it, why make an identical ledger?" I was on me feet pacing.

Sonya ran her fingers over it again. She flipped pages and then flipped them back. When she looked up at me, her eyes were round and bright. "Eureka!"

"Okay, what'ya you got?" I plopped down next to her on the couch.

"See here," she pointed, "Drexel, Stanley." I followed her painted nail along the name column of truck drivers. "They're all last name first until you get to Greg, Thompson. There are six names that are first name first."

"Yeah, so he gets dyslexic sometimes."

"Well, if you cross reference the names Henry put in, first names first; you get guys that wrecked during delivery." Her mouth was open like a puppy waiting for a treat.

"The ledger Jeffers gave me listed all last names first."

Sonya kept flipping through pages furiously. "Look here, this guy Sam Jenkins has a star next to his name."

"Good work doll. That's where we'll start." Our smiles wiped clean off when the sound of two car doors opening and closing crept into our ears. I held a finger to my lips and walked to the window. Flat against the wall I stuck an eye out the side of the curtain peering into the street. I could see the back end of a large black sedan, the one that had picked me up last night.

I reached under my coat and felt the comfort of the iron I had tucked away. Sonya shook her head no. She stepped quietly to the kitchen then came back a little quicker.

Her soft hand touched mine. In a whisper she said, "We can get out the kitchen window."

I frowned, looking for a fight, and then flipped the lock on the door to give us some time.

I had her out the window when I heard the door handle jiggle. I popped my head out the window and saw Sonya hanging from the gutter. Her fingers released and she dropped a few feet to the concrete. I scuttled out the window just as the door smashed open.

We hot-footed it down the drive. I looked back as I got to the curb to see Careep standing at the top of the stairs. He reached under his coat and pulled that canon of his. I reached in my front pocket and pulled my pocketknife. He smiled for the first time. I smiled back then knelt by the rear tire of the sedan. I took a gamble he would not shoot and cut the valve stem on the tire. Careep blundered down the rickety stairs with the driver close behind. We were to my truck, pulling away before they made it to the street.

Sonya had her face pushed against the glass, watching them disappear as we rounded the corner. She turned to me, smiling, and let out a roar. "That was tops Cotton. Did you see the look on that ape's face?" she let out a laugh. I did not repress the smile that pushed out showing my full bite.

The flat tire would put some distance between Jeffers's thugs and us. I wasn't worried about Careep after the showing this morning in the warehouse office. Sure, he would be on the attack, and might bring a little fire, but my confidence was up. With Sonya at my side, a little nugget was growing deep in my gut. It was a familiar feeling but also all new. I shoved it deeper, forcing my mind to forget it.

We bounced along brick roads until hitting asphalt. I cut a left and hurried along a few blocks before turning up Mills road. We took it the long way to Orange Avenue. I just wanted to make sure we put some distance between the henchmen and us.

"Where to now, fella?" Sonya said with spunk in her voice, as she watched the store fronts pass by heading north. Adrenaline continued to pump behind her eyes.

"I'm taking you to your hotel."

She pouted. Her lower lip pushed out and she gripped both bare knees. "Awe, come on Cotton that was fun."

"Too much fun for one day. Best thing for you to do now is hang low at the hotel. I recommend staying in and ordering room service."

"You really think those men will be looking for me?" Lines formed in her brow as the weight of the situation dropped on her.

"Sure. You're part of this now. I would feel safer if you kept quiet at the hotel. I can swing back by and pick you up for dinner." My eyes darted her way. I saw her smile as I reached out and touched her hand. She gripped it the rest of the ride.

The hotel was quiet this time of year. Just after Christmas it would pick up as snow birds migrated south by the carloads to thaw out. It was just a stop over, a night or two at most, on their way to the white sandy beaches of coastal towns like Saint Pete or Fort Meyers. Tourists often meant collaborating jobs. Other private detectives or law offices would call me up out of the book and ask me to locate a woman, usually late twenties with recently dyed blond hair. I just had to report back or meet the detective when he arrived. It was easy dough.

We swung into the round-about in front of the Orange Court Hotel. It was a nice enough place. Four stories in a squared horse shoe shape. A kid in his late teens grabbed my door. I gave him a couple bucks and told him to keep it running close by. Sonya and I walked in together. Polished marble floors with deep wood grain trim and lots of brass accents adorned the lobby. Plush velvet chairs dotted the floor of the empty lobby. A balding little round man behind the desk was sorting letters when we walked up to the counter.

"How may I help you?" he did not bother to look up. I popped the bell on the desk and his head snapped up, showing off a thin mustache. Sonya giggled into her hand. He frowned then forced a smile. I read his nametag.

"Jon, Ms. Clementine would like to check in. You can do that can't you?" I pinched my eyes and curled the corners of my mouth while leaning in over the high counter. Jon's round face dropped three shade of white as he peeled back. His bowling pin body nearly tipped as he went back on his heels. I shifted my face into a smile once I had his full attention.

"Why yes, of course I can handle that ah... Mister, ah...." Sweat dewed across his high forehead.

"Sonya Clementine is her name." I smiled bringing him back on his flat feet. Jon tugged at the bottom of his charcoal grey jacket held together by distressed brass buttons running up the center. Jon went about the business of checking Sonya in. He gave her a key and told her the luggage had arrived earlier and was already in her room. He tried again to get my name, explaining it was for safety reasons. I flashed him my investigators badge and that shut him up and increased his perspiration.

Sonya and I took the stairs to the third floor, prolonging our time together. Along the way our conversation turned light. It was her second trip to Florida but her first in my town. On her first trip to see the ocean, she fell in love with it and could not see a reason to come to Florida and not visit the beach. The miles of pine broken up with groves was growing on her and she looked forward to seeing more of the town. We stood in front of her door. She held the key in both hands.

"I'll be back by in a couple of hours, to make sure you're settled in." I held her shoulder for assurance. Her skin was soft and smooth against my rough fingertips. A waft of lavender and vanilla fired parts of my brain that had suffocated in bourbon for too long. Her red lips parted just enough to see the white caps of her teeth and I had tunnel vision. I wanted to experience her moist lips pressing against mine. Her whispered breath stopped and there was complete silence. We melted together.

The key fell a million miles from her hand crashing to the carpeted floor and shattered like crystal as my focus fractured. I blinked a couple of times before releasing her; her eyes half- closed, as if she were coming out of a deep sleep. Her head remained tilted slightly as she leaned into me. I wanted to tell her to stop and snap out of it, but I wasn't snapping out of anything anytime soon. I pulled her into me tight with a force that knocked her hat off and together we crashed into the locked hotel room door.

After a couple of rounds I pulled back, looked at her bottomless coffee colored eyes, and took a deep breath. Sonya let out a half-laugh and ran a few fingers through her hair.

"Let's get you inside." I said and grabbed up the key.

Inside, the room smelled of lemons from a can. The bed was a double with two suitcases on top. A desk was in the corner with a telephone on it and beyond that, the window. I pulled the heavy drapes back to let in some Florida sunshine. From the third floor, you could see a mile out across the flat landscape. A few buildings poked up through the tree canopy.

Sonya was coming out of the bathroom when I turned from the window. She was pushing back a curl that managed to break free from the other curls and invade her flushed face.

"I hate to kiss and run Sonya but I still have a job to do for your brother." I watched her face drop as a pale whiteness filtered out the rouge.

"Can't I go with you, Cotton?"

"I'm sorry, not this time. Get some rest. There's been plenty of excitement for the both of us today." I tried to keep my voice gentle. I was out of practice talking sweet to girls.

I moved past her, fighting the urge to continue what we had in the hall. I said, "Why don't you see about cashing that check Jeffers gave you. If this case is going where I think it is - the check might have enough rubber in it to bounce all the way to outer space."

"Okay Cotton. I'll arrange the funds with the hotel manager." She put her eyes down. The last thing I would have thought this morning was that by lunch I would be falling for some dame, a dead client's sister no less. My head was so far off track leaving my eyes in fixed positions on her body. Blowing off the rest of the day and spending it there in the room until dawn would be just fine with me. Then her resemblance to Henry hit me like a bullet, reminding me why I could not let things cool. She rung her hands and wiped sweaty palms on her thighs. I reached out and plucked her chin with my finger.

"Rest up. I'll be back in a couple of hours and we can get some dinner. How does that sound?"

She smiled then shoved me out of the room, "It takes a girl time to get ready for a date."

I whistled a light tune all the way out of the hotel.

***

The valet was quick to open the door of my idling International. I slid in, pulled out of the U shaped drive and headed south on Orange Ave. Both ledgers sat on the seat next to me. We counted six different accidents involving six different drivers. Only one of them did I ever recall reading in the paper. A truck loaded with grapefruit had faulty breaks and ran a signal, plowing into a school bus. No one was killed; the bus was empty on its way back to the yard after dropping all the kids off. The bus driver was hurt and taken to a hospital.

I swung the pickup over and parked crooked with the bed hanging out in the street. I scrambled to a pay phone and dropped a dime in. I asked to be connected to Robert Gomez at the Sentinel.

The phone rang a dozen times. The operator butted in and asked if I wanted to keep trying, I told her to do it. On the seventh ring, I finally heard his voice, "Hello, Gomez here."

"Bobby, it's your ole pal Chamberlain." I heard his heavy breath through the line. Bobby and I went way back. Along the way, we had good times and bad, like any relationship. The last time we helped each other out, it did not end well for the reporter. He received threats from the bad guys and got hassled by the good guys, nearly fracturing his relationship with city hall. Since city hall was his beat, he never wanted to hear from me again.

"Shit, Cotton what do you want?" he lit a cigarette and blew it through the phone.

[52]

"I need you to look into something for me."

"That was kind of a rhetorical question. Last time I helped you out for a scoop, I ended up nearly losing my job not to mention my life. You know they got security here now. You need an ID badge to get up to my floor, thanks to you."

"Yeah, but did we or did we not put some bad guys away and help out a family in need?"

"You did. I lost an exclusive." I could tell he was sitting. Only one phone rang in the back and no one was shouting. It was a slow news cycle, so I used it to hook him.

"This is big time Bobby. I'm telling it to you over the phone. Just look into the archives on some accidents with Jeffers's shipping trucks." Bobby's whistle pierced my eardrum. I had him good. I rattled off the names and dates of each accident then told him I would meet him in half an hour. He agreed and hung up.

My coat was off and my sleeves rolled up. I had the windows down and a dry seventy-eight degree breeze circulated the cab. It was late in the day and the sun began to dip below the buildings, casting long shadows and creating cold spots for the coming night. Ducking Christmas shoppers, I cut through Robinson over to Magnolia and back to my office. I needed to clean up and change my clothes for when I saw Sonya tonight. I had not changed my suit in three days. It was one of those weeks.

It was the second right I took, when I spotted the pearl white Plymouth sedan two car lengths behind. This city is not large and chances are we we're all headed in the same direction. This car was familiar. First I spotted it passing by while on the phone with Bobby. Now it was on my ass. If I was right, then this fool saved me a lot of legwork tracking her down. Looking through the side mirrors, I tried to get a good look at the driver. All I could make out was the outline of a dark hat. I weaved the truck a little, glancing occasionally and hoping for a better angle. The more I weaved the further back he drifted. Around a bend, I could see a dame riding shotgun. Dark hair and a dark hat for her as well. It was not much of description and nothing to go on. I took out my pistol and slipped it under my thigh.

I threw on my blinker, cut a hard right onto Pine Street and kept the momentum going into a parking lot. The Plymouth stopped on the corner. I watched it creep by then speed off down the road. I started after it, but stopped at the gate. A prowl car sat crooked, parked illegally. In my gut, I knew an officer of the law was sitting in my office.

The door to my office was open. I went in.

"Hello Lieutenant Blake. You must be climbing high in the ranks to have a chauffeur." I hung my jacket and my rod on the hall tree. Blake was sitting on the couch with a coke bottle about half full of chew and spit. The patrolman, who drove, stood in the corner with his hands neatly folded behind his back looking statuesque in his dark blue uniform and spit shined shoes.

Blake looked at me with tired eyes. "Don't give me any of your horse noodles," I smirked at the Lieutenant's substitute for curse words. It only angered him. "My car ran into a ditch during a pursuit of two men in a black

[54]

sedan seen leaving Henry Clementine's place." He grumbled and looked down at mud caked shoes.

"Did they get away?" I sat on the corner of the desk and lit a smoke.

"Yeah. A witness said a man and a pretty little woman were seen coming and going just before those two men were. Happen to know anything about that?" He scraped his shoes together leaving a pile of grey powder on my office floor.

"A woman, huh?" I got up and snubbed out the cigarette. "You'll have to talk while I walk. I need to get cleaned up." I went to a tall metal filing cabinet. From the top drawer came folded dark blue suit pants, a pair of underwear and some fresh socks. I entered the holding cell closet and slipped into the fresh clothes. I grabbed a shirt off a hanger and picked out a tie.

"Damn it Cotton, are you living here?"

I nodded and slipped the tie into a double Windsor.

"This building ain't zoned for that. I could get you tossed outta here." Blake leaned forward and pushed himself off the leather couch. He slanted his stout frame against the door jam of the cell.

"This mystery couple at Henry's place, did your witness get a description?" I changed shoes in there as well.

"Nah, but they ran off in a red pickup truck. Now, who do we know with a red pickup truck?" Blake scratched the stubble on his round jaw. He reached in his pocket and pulled a tin of chew. He plucked a pinch and stuffed it between his lower lip and gum. His eyes slanted and a vertical crease broke his eyebrows in two. I frowned at him.

"Don't know. The registration for my pickup says burnt orange."

Blake rubbed a hand across his face. "Now Cotton, don't make me start cursing, it's a habit I can't easily break."

"Okay Blake, lets play twenty questions. I'll go first. Did you put a tail on me?"

He blinked a couple times then kneaded his hands together. He wished he had but I could tell he did not.

"Okay you're turn." I said, tucking my fresh shirt into clean slacks.

"What did you find at Clementine's that we missed?" From the corner of his eye he scanned my desk, looking over the top of it for any open files or folders.

"Nothing."

"You mean to tell me…" He bit his lip then dribbled spit in to his coke bottle. The devil's words worked their way out in a muted mumble. Then he said, "Okay what else you want to know?"

"Nothing else."

"That's it? Either you are the world's worst detective -"

"I know you have nothing else. You don't have the guys from Henry's break-in or know what they took, or else you would have called me down to the station, and if you had the blond witness, you would have called me down as well. Now I have a date to get ready for." I nodded to them both and left.

It was a few blocks to the paper, so I walked it. Driving would be a hassle and I wanted to stop and get flowers on the way back. Walking was easier. I went out the back and hunched down along side a dumpster. My building was one in from the corner, so I had a good view of the cross street. Sitting near the intersection parked, was the pearl sedan. Both passengers sat looking at my building. They were in a good spot to see me come out the front and could get behind my truck no matter the direction I went. I darted between cars, cutting through the parking lot until I got to my truck. I retrieved Henry's secret ledger, sticking it in the back of my waistband. I cut back up the alley and headed north on foot. I left them sitting.

The inside of the paper building was swanky. Dark green marble with swirls of white checkered the floor and heavy wood accents with lots of brass trim made me feel like I was in a bank. In the middle of the large hall was a circular wooden island. Two men in midnight blue security uniforms stood directing people. Along the south wall, a row of teller windows encased in wood and brass held women taking in all the public notices; births, deaths, and wedding announcements. On the north end were elevators. I made for them when the guard called out.

"Can I help you, sir?" He had a northern accent that was out of place. He was large, with a square jaw and deep-set eyes separated by a hooked nose. The other guard was skinny, his uniform hung on him as if on a clothes hanger.

"I came to see Bobby Gomez."

[57]

"You have to sign in - then I call him." He pushed a clipboard my way and picked up a black phone receiver. He spoke into it and we waited. He nodded and mumbled a 'yes' then hung up.

"Here's your badge." He scribbled Bobby's name on the badge just below the printed word "Visitor". I pinned it to my jacket.

I met Bobby in the hall of the fourth floor. Bobby was tall and lean, with hard to control black hair spiraling out above the temples. He was in his late twenties, with a pale yellow complexion that would turn a shiny copper from April through November. His family went way back in Florida history, claiming to have arrived with Ponce de Leon, more than likely, not. However, his family owned thousands of acres just south of town and raised cattle for generations. We greeted and he ushered me back to an archives room. The room was lined floor to ceiling with metal bookshelves. On each shelf was a book labeled with a month and a year. There were other books, mostly with titles about Florida in them. I ran my finger along the spines as we walked to the back of the poorly lit archives room.

A bright light was coming from the back corner of the room. Bobby looked back at me, "Don't worry sifting through all this. We have it all on microfilm." His cracker accent was more evident in person than over the phone. I knew him since he was a punk kid and I was not much older or wiser. His accent thinned after he got back from college. Now it only showed when he was excited or in a hurry.

Bobby dragged a squealing chair over and we sat in front of the microfilm. The images whisked by, blurring as they went. He pulled up one article, dated eight months ago. He scanned aloud the contents, "A Jeffers's Produce truck driven by Darren Gravelet collided with…" Bobby continued scrolling. "…Justin Daniels, driver of the Jeffers Produce truck broke through a guard rail along 17-92… the cause of the crash - faulty brakes. It was all investigated by the county sheriffs. This is just two cases. You said ya' had six." Bobby was getting excited; his cracker accent was bleeding through the educated one.

I reached behind to my lower back and pulled the ledger. I opened it and flipped pages until I found one marked with the reverse of names listed. "Here." I said pointing at Jake McCollum. Bobby flipped through the microfilm to the days after the accident, nothing. We tried again and still nothing. I pinched my lips together letting air leak out the corner of my mouth. Bobby took the ledger and thumbed through it.

"Who insures Jeffers's trucks?" Bobby asked without picking his nose out of the book.

"Not sure." I murmured, not having run down that angle. "I figured self-insured."

Bobby leaned back in his chair and rubbed his hands over his pale face. He slapped his knees and stood up, saying, "Damn you, Chamberlain. You bring me the scent and this dog is on the hunt, but I need more." He was pulling sayings from his culture.

"I thought of you first." I gave him a toothy grin.

Bobby sat back down. He straightened out his tie before saying, "If he's self-insured then the accidents aren't for the payouts."

Bobby Gomez had a point. Four out of the six accidents went unreported to the news. There was no record other than that of an investigator on the Jeffers's payroll. I leaned forward in my seat and cupped my chin with both hands. Staring at my tapping foot, I knew there had to be a tie in between the accidents and Jeffers. Henry Clementine was tracking something in his books that got him plugged with two slugs. Now I had a tail, and it was not one of Jeffers's crew.

"Thanks for all your effort. I'll leave you the ledgers, maybe there is more in there." I said, standing. "I have to go see about a girl, but I promise to call you when this thing breaks." I extended my right hand to Bobby.

He took it saying, "Yeah, you better after what happened last time. You owe me a hundred stories like this. I'll keep looking into this, though." His college accent was back. I made for the door, while he began sifting through the ledgers.

I handed over my visitor badge to the square faced guard and hit the street. Walking the four blocks back to my office, I stopped off at a florist. It was a small shop with a cute young girl in a green apron. I figured I could not go wrong with an arrangement of six roses and six tulips. After the purchase, I went back through the alley and peered around the corner. The Plymouth sat in the same spot with the same two dopes staring with bored looks on their faces. The woman's hat came off and she fluffed shiny brown hair. I thought back to what the pervert cabbie told me through broken teeth. Anger swelled in my stomach. My left eye pinched a little. With determination, I walked across the street, flowers in hand.

Traffic was filling up the street with men who wanted to get home to their wives. The light was red and cars piled up a dozen deep in both lanes. I cut through the momentary parking lot and walked right up the passenger door. I held the flowers in one hand and my gun in the other.

The dame turned and jerked her head up looking me in the face. She let out a yip and the man next to her spun in his seat. I kept the gun just out of view of the nosey couple. The guy fumbled in his waist band and pulled a policeman's issue .38. It was black and worn blue at the edges. I could see rust congregating on a couple of the cylinders. He would more than likely blow himself up before he ever shot me. I brought my iron around in plain view. He dropped his pistol to the floor of the car.

The guy twisted the key in the ignition in an attempt to escape. Over the roar of the engine, I shouted for him to kill it before I killed him.

The driver's face was long and a second chin bulged under his slacked jaw. His hair was gone at the crown; the remaining hair was an ash blonde and wavy. He was dressed in blue jeans and a faded denim shirt. He killed the engine and sat with both hands on the wheel. The woman hollered at him for giving up so fast, saying, "Sam! You dimwit!" She looked back at me with the gun a couple feet from her face and settled down.

I recognized her right away, as our eyes locked. My first impression had been right, without all that makeup and wig she was a decent looking girl. I got into the back seat.

"Nice to see you again, Willimina." I said. Sam's eyes puffed out so far I thought they would float away.

"And you," I jabbed the pistol deep into the back of the front seat prodding the driver, "I got to the scene soon enough to see you drive off after shooting Henry Clementine." Sam started to interrupt me with some babble. I cut him off. "On second thought, you couldn't have shot Henry." Sam's shoulders relaxed. "No, not you. You lack the steel it takes to kill a guy. I should know, I've done it often enough." There have been plenty of shootouts in the years I bounty hunted and private-eyed, but the truth was I only had two deaths on my hands. The hate for Henry's killer was festering, and I wanted to make it three.

Sam spoke up, stuttering at first, "We didn't keel nobody... I swear." He had a strong local Cracker accent.

"Okay, what was *she* doing talking to Henry before he was shot?" I leaned forward from the back seat nearly sticking my head between the two. Willimina twisted in the seat, putting her back to the door.

"Sam dropped me at the corner. I just wanted to talk to Henry and... and plead with him to..." She got teary eyed, and then the damn broke. Her hands covered her face as her body bounced. "It was so awful."

Sam tried to comfort her. I snapped the pistol at him and said, "Not yet." He slid back to his side of the car.

"What was it you wanted Henry to do for you?"

Sam found his voice, "Last year, my grove, Butterfield Groves, was hit hard from the frost. We lost half our crop and nearly a third of our trees. The dues for the warehouse went up this year, and we just couldn't cover it."

Willimina butted in, "You must know all this, right? You're working for them." Her voice was stern and tears had faded. With the two of them side by side, I noticed something about Willimina I had skipped in our first encounter: she was not a Florida native.

A falling leaf could have toppled me at that moment. These two were no hit men and probably could not have even intimidated old, nervous guy Henry.

"If I'm working for them, and I guess you mean Jeffers, then why where you following me?" I eased off with the gun, slipping it back in under my coat.

"To plead with you to back off." Sam hollered. "No one else has to die over this."

Sam started to explain the ins and outs of orange growing to me, but I cut him off. "Look, you two, I have nothing to do with it." I said. Sam looked pitiful and at his wits end. His scared fumbling tactics shed new light on this case for me. It was Willimina I couldn't get an angle on.

"You're a liar, Mr. Cotton, nothing but a hired gun and a liar." Hate filled her mocha eyes, glassing them over and sending a chill down my spine.

"You got this all wrong sister. Henry hired me to look into Jeffers's dealings. He said there was something screw bally going on that would sooner or later involve the law. He didn't want to be implicated in any wrong doing, so he hired me." I settled back in the seat.

"Then why did you go to visit Clinton Jeffers yesterday?" This broad was good. I might have a job for her if she ever cools off.

"Just who the hell are you, Willimina? I mean really, you're not from around here. Are you a lawyer for the growers?" I lit a smoke.

"My mistake Mr. Cotton, you're not a liar, you're just dumb." Her eyes pulled together, and her cheeks sucked in. She was getting pleasure in all this and I found that look of hers that was missing.

It was in that cold stare that I saw it, "Ms. Jeffers, does father know the company you keep?"

Her eyes peeled back, then relaxed int. While she found her cool, I lost mine. My heart was thumping in my chest and my leg started to bounce.

She said, "About time.", and turned back around in her seat.

"Just what's your beef in all this Ms. Jeffers?"

She turned to me slowly. Her eyes narrowed. "I was away at college, then traveled for sometime now." She paused and reached out a hand that touched the side of my arm before continuing. "When I got back a few months ago, things around the depot had changed. My father was taking meetings with shady men from south Florida, and then the accidents started happening. I found one man I could trust, and that was Henry Clementine. He was onto something and it got him killed. I brought Sam here to convince you to help us." There was genuine concern in her voice.

I pressed on, "Who threatened you about the warehouse fees?"

"First it was the phone calls, then a couple of fellas come to the house. They started harassin' us and our workers." Sam said.

"Were they Jeffers men?"

"Never saw 'em before. Dark skinned, looked sorta Spanish or Italian and talked like they were from South Florida." Sam looked to the corner of his eye as he recanted the details.

"Are any of the other growers having similar problems?"

"Oh, and how!" Sam perked up. He put both hands on the back of the seat and said, "The Parkers and the Taylors both had trouble. The Westermans had one of their trucks catch fire. They ruled it a faulty fuel line but two days before they were visited by the Spanish fellas."

"Are you familiar with Gravelet and Daniels?"

"Yeah, a couple of drivers, only those weren't accidents." Sam shook his head.

"Have you talked to the other growers about this harassment?"

Sam balled his fist and tapped it against the steering wheel. "We had it set up for today, but then Henry was shot. Everyone got spooked and backed out."

"Why not sell the fruit south, or west in Polk County?" I knew there had to be something stopping these growers from just skipping Jeffers altogether, but I needed to hear it from them.

"Unions and …" Sam looked down at his lap, "the law. Mr. Jeffers has the Sheriff's Department in his pocket. We have to go through him, or we don't go at all." He sighed. The man was defeated.

The worst thing in the world is a dirty cop. Someone sworn to protect people and make them feel safe, using the weapons granted to him by the people on the people. My heart rate quickened again as I squeezed down on the flowers meant for a girl who just lost her brother to greed. My focus was trained now on a rich man who only wanted more, and liked to trample on the little guy to get it. With this information, I was starting to put a picture together that allowed my mind to catch up to what my gut had known all along: Clinton Jeffers, dirt bag extraordinaire. If that warehouse was not so important to the local growers of this county, I'd have set fire to it right then. The grin across my face would stretch from both coasts of this state. Then I would go after Jeffers. If he has the county in his pocket, I would have to tread lightly for awhile, but at least I knew one honest cop. Blake and I might not have been best buds, but we trusted each other.

"Okay you two, just go on back to the farm. I want you to talk to the other growers and, if there are anymore attempts on your lives, contact me or get in touch with Lieutenant Blake at Homicide. Got it?"

They solemnly nodded in sequence. Willimina synchronized eyes with me just for a moment. In that flash, I got a tingle down my spine, the kind that lets you know you are a man. I jumped out of the car and ran up to my office. I had the operator patch me through to the Orange Court Hotel and up to Sonya's room. It rang a handful of times before she answered.

"Hello." Her voice was sweet, even out of a dead sleep. I could hear her strain as she stretched out on the bed.

"Sorry honey, did I wake you?"

[66]

"Hhmm, its okay. I just laid down for a minute and must have really passed out." She let out a yawn.

"Listen kid, I need to give you a rain check on dinner."

She dropped a bogus whimper on me. "Is it about the case, Cotton?"

"Sure is. Did you cash that check?"

"Yes, the bank manager was very friendly when he saw Jeffers's name on it. He said it would still take a couple days to clear and he would wire it to my bank back home. He fronted me a thousand and I put it in the hotel safe."

"Good girl. I want you to lay low tonight. Order in or something. I'll be by later tonight to see you." Business over pleasure, if only she had come into my life sooner.

"Okay Cotton, I'll be a good girl...for now." She hung up. That last part really got me and I was ready to ditch this case and get down to the Orange Court and see how they do up in Indiana.

I dropped the receiver and wondered how two siblings could be so very different. I was happy it turned out the way it had. The thoughts did not last but a second when the phone rang.

"Go ahead." I said dryly.

"Chamberlain, its Bobby. Listen I kinda went over you and called around about the insurance company myself." He had a twinge of excitement in his voice masked with a little repentance.

"Go on." This case was heating up and I was barely working it.

"So the policy owner is not local, it's a firm out of Miami, called Miami Trust Insurance." The ties to Miami were glowing red-hot. "Here's the kicker, the first accident was self-insured, Jeffers paid out himself. Jeffers then got insurance last year."

I did not need Bobby to finish his thought; my head was wrapped around this tight. I could see the finish line. "And soon, after all the accidents started." I said bluntly.

"You nailed it Cotton."

"Do me another favor Bobby," I said.

"At this point, anything."

"Follow up on the drivers in accidents after the insurance. Let's see what the payouts were to them."

"I gotcha. This hound is on the hunt." Bobby's cracker accent was thicker than ever when I got off the line with him.

I next put in a call to Lieutenant Blake's desk. There was no answer. I tried again through the main line and got a copper behind a desk. He was short on his answers, as if he had something better to do. He said Blake was out. I left him instructions to have Blake call me right away, that is was about the Clementine murder. I was growing anxious and wanted to rush out to Jeffers's place right away, go in fists blazing and get some real answers out of the guy. News papers and politicians alike heralded Clinton Jeffers as a pillar of our community. An innovator and investor that helped build our central Florida county into something more than alligators and orange groves. Now he was taking advantage of the very people that worked to make him what he was. I wanted to shake him by the ankles until every last penny fell from his pockets.

I poured a drink to take the edge off until Blake could call back. I wheeled my chair over next to the couch and propped my feet up. I could see out the window better from here and watched the people below scurry about, taking care of grocery lists and electric bills. A couple kids rode by on bikes hollering to each other. It was great weather out. Floridians treated winter like folks up north treated summer. We came out to play November through March; the rest of the year was spent trying to stay cool indoors anywhere that has an air conditioner.

The burning orange sun dipped westward. A few cotton-filled clouds began to flush with pink as the sky beyond turned a deep blue. The air itself began to look charged with pink particles, as the neon colored sky reflected off building windows, casting the entire city in shades of pastel pink. I leaned back in my chair and sipped my bourbon. My eyes, like the sun, dipped into darkness. I escaped to the image of Sonya's face.

A light knock sounded at my office door and gradually grew louder as my sleep-filled mind organized thoughts to get me out of this late afternoon coma. My head turned, expecting a familiar face to let himself in. My office was now pitch-dark. Through the frosted pane, I could make out two dark shapes like phantoms in the night. I had to rub the sleep from my eyes to make sure they were not.

I flipped on the light as I opened the door wide. Two men, olive skinned with black hair in dark suits, and hats pulled low over hungry eyes stood before me. Their arms were held together by clasping palms. Two sets of dark eyes looked me up and down. I felt like a runway model with a medium-rare steak around my neck. The one to my left was a head taller; the other barely came up to my chin. We made the perfect Russian dolls. I wished I was still dreaming, but when the little one brushed passed me I knew I was fully awake.

Closing the door behind them, I said, "Mi casa es su casa."

The little guy spoke first, "Nice place." Cuban. He walked around taking inventory of everything he saw, the cell door; my rod hanging like art off the coat rack a dozen feet from where I stood. "My name is Raulo. This is my associate, Vinny." Vinny nodded, but unlike his roving counterpart, held statuesque next to me.

"What can I do for the two of you?" I moved towards my hanging pistol. Vinny casually stepped between us. "No," Vinny said with a distinct Northern urban sound, totally different than his associate.

Raulo continued to pace like a caged carnivore around my office as he spoke. "It is my understanding that you were hired under false pretenses. Your client's employer would like to rescind those services. He was under the false impression that something, shall we say, shady was going on."

"Yeah, a whole lot of shadows are being cast these days."

Raulo's face went taught. He jerked his head towards me, as if I pulled it on a string. "Let's just agree everything is where it should be. Huh?"

Vinny stepped forward and untangled his meaty hands. A small pistol with a large circumference barrel shimmered in the sixty-watt bulb. He sucked his teeth repeatedly, sounding like a clock.

I was never very good at gambling. I would change my bet at the last minute because the number four dog took a shit before the race. I went back to the track for that thrill of laying down a couple bucks at the window, hoping it turned into hundreds. I could read people better than I could read dogs. Raulo and Vinny were not going to leave without something.

I kicked Vinny, toe to hand, and the gun dropped. I took a wild swing that connected but did not carry much weight. I spun, as Raulo lunged towards me with his hat off and head down. His right shoulder connected square in my belly, his arms wrapping around my waist. I let my feet slide back and then squared them. I hooked my arms around his doubled over waist, interlocking my fingers and allowing his momentum to aid in lifting his feet off the floor. He crashed onto the top of my desk and rolled off. Vinny clocked me across the side of my face and I felt my knees tingle, but I managed to stay up. His second throw was wide, leaving him open for a quick jab with my left. I followed it up with a right pop.

Raulo was back on his feet and charging again. I side stepped him and pushed him into the couch. Vinny turned his large frame around, raising balled fists. All I could see was a bulky gold ring dancing before me. He jabbed and I bobbed. He threw a wide right, and I lifted a knee to his midsection. Vinny recoiled quickly. Raulo was on his feet as the two backed me in the corner of my office.

Raulo reached into his back pocket, pulling a sap, saying, "We came to deliver a message to stay the hell away from Jeffers Depot."

Vinny dove in for a bear hug. I struggled against the big lug, throwing wild fists and kicks. He took the blows like a champ. Raulo stepped in over him and swung the sap down, connecting to the side of my head, just behind my ear. Electricity fired through every nerve ending. I could feel every hair follicle on my body. My head began to feel like a hundred pounds on a rubber neck. My knees buckled and I fell flat.

Raulo stood over me, as my eyes rolled like marbles in their sockets. "Stay out of this, Dick."

As the pair left the office, the last thing I heard was the phone ringing. I could not make out if it was in my head or the one on the desk. It did not matter; I was not getting up to answer it. A deep still black lake was waiting out there before me and all I had to do was jump in. I did not hesitate.

CHAPTER 5

I was floating in darkness, my mind empty of thought and at totally at rest. Then a babbling started, slowly rising in volume. The pitch changed from high to low. Images of the last couple of days flashed by as light filtered through the blackness. I felt warmth on my face then a cool dampness over my forehead. I blinked a few times before I was fully capable of keeping my eyes open.

Sonya had my head resting on her lap. Her hand was warm as it slowly stroked the side of my face. A cool cloth draped over my forehead and an icepack was tucked behind my ear. From the corner of my eye, I saw a round solid shape propped against my desk. Blake was barking into the phone, calling for an ambulance and shouting my address. He repeated "officer down" to the operator.

I looked up at Sonya's tired wet eyes, "I'm okay kid."

Through light sobs she said, "Thank God you have a thick skull." Then she touched my face once more. Her breath had a faint smell of whiskey.

"Bobby called me looking for you, so I called the hotel and Sonya said she had been calling you. I called here and no answer. We all kinda met up and found you on the floor. Sonya was so shaken up I had her drink some of your punch over there." Blake hiked a thumb towards the desk. I looked up at Sonya and she smiled back.

Bobby came through the door with a paper cup filled with cold water. Sonya took it from him asking me to sip it.

"Don't get up just yet." Blake said with a wad of tobacco in his lip. "Now tell us what in tar nation went on here?" He spat into a coke bottle.

"He doesn't have to answer questions right now Lieutenant, let the man rest." Sonya spat a little of her own.

I grabbed the back cushion of the couch and pulled up. I was woozy and felt I might vomit. I kept the acid down and said, "Its okay honey. Blake's right. The sooner I talk the sooner we get the bastards." It took a few seconds to collect my thoughts and communicate them logically. The time line was a little fuzzy of the two men coming in and what they said when they said it, before my lights went out. I managed to get it all out there.

Sonya shook with anger and cursed Clinton Jeffers name. I pulled her into me and ran my hand across her back.

"It isn't all Jeffers's doing." I said catching myself up along with the rest of the day I just had.

"This thing runs deep." Bobby jumped in. He went on to explain to Blake and Sonya the trail we were on with the insurance scam and the ties to a Miami based company with Coposey mob ties. The mob tie-in was new to me but not a far leap after considering Raulo and Vinny. I piped in with what Willimina and Sam confessed to me in the car.

When I let on about the County Sheriffs blocking growers from getting around Jeffers's depot, I thought

Lieutenant Blake was going to blow a gasket. He pinched his eyes tight and curled his upper lip. He wrenched out the wad of chew and tossed it in the garbage pale.

"I hate dirty cops. Damn it, I hate 'em." Blake pounded a fist into my oak desk. We sat in silence while he went with a lot of talk of kicking ass and taking names. Once he calmed to a low murmur we drew a picture linking the corruption in Orange County and the state.

A siren echoed through the buildings lining the street below.

"Looks like your ride is here." Bobby chuckled, the first smile between any of us.

"Oh no, I'm not going to a hospital. You'll take care of me, won't you Sonya." I said.

Before Sonya could reply through her smile, Blake rebuked, "You're going to see a doctor, Cotton. Your brains got scrambled earlier. I need you healthy."

"Sonya here used to be a nurse." I gave Sonya a wink.

"I'll take good care of him Lieutenant, I swear it." She wrapped her arms around me; almost head butting me in the same spot I had been sapped.

Doc Keenan busted through the door, followed by two men in white coats and half a dozen police officers. The street below was lit up like a Christmas parade. Red and blue lights flashed and circled the tops of black and white cars. Blake ushered the other officers out shouting for them to make way.

Doc Keenan dropped a black leather bag and took a knee in front of me. Digging into his doctor's bag he said, "Hell, Cotton, the call came in like you were dead or something worse." His breath was hot with whiskey adding to my need to vomit. He went on to say in a low tone, "These two are from Wilson's Funeral Home, come to pick you up." Doc pulled a flashlight and sent a beam in my eye. I tried to blink and look away. He tilted my head and looked at the bruise as well as the one on my face.

Looking me in the eyes he said in a soft voice, "Can you walk?"

I nodded and stood up. Doc barked over his shoulder, "Go on and get outta here you vultures."

The two men in white dropped their heads and wheeled out the gurney they had in tow.

"I'm not going to any hospital." I grumbled.

Doc Keenan began to protest, all the while keeping his voice in an eerie calm. Blake finally stepped in and lead on that Sonya had been a nurse and would take charge of my care. Doc Keenan gave her a once over as if he were going to find credentials pinned on her somewhere. He reached into his black bag and pulled a bottle of pills.

"I'm sure you're aware the signs of a concussion nurse." He shook the bottle at her. "Take as needed." He said in a huff and walked out. I could not blame the guy for being sore. He had left his barstool for no reason.

Blake went right back to business once Doctor Keenan left. "Cotton, what you are implicating here about the county sheriffs and probably the county mayor could have major repercussions. And this goes for you too, Bobby," Blake wagged a finger at the both of us. "I'm going to take this up with the city mayor tomorrow, and even the governor. Now I've got sixteen years on the force which means I either make captain soon or I retire. Understand where I'm going?"

Wagner

I nodded. He ordered the both of us, like a father to his sons, to lay low and keep quiet until we had all the facts. When he was done, Bobby offered to walk out with Blake. I liked Blake. He was a man of few words and never of them curses unless I was involved. We had known each other for going on ten years and formed a good working relationship.

"I'm taking you to the hotel." Sonya said throwing my arm over her shoulder as her arm went around my waist. With my free arm, I grabbed the bottle of rye and slipped it in my pocket. We went down the elevator and out to my truck. Bobby waved so long as he got into his car. Blake hustled his round body over to help as Sonya slipped me in the passenger seat.

"One other thing Cotton, get some rest. After tomorrow, you're gonna need it." He slapped the fender of my truck. I gave him a three finger solute and watched him direct the traffic jam of cops out of the street. Sonya got in behind the wheel.

"Can you drive this thing?"

"A farm girl like me? It would be embarrassing if I couldn't." She smiled and pecked me on the forehead. It hurt like hell but I smiled through the pain.

CHAPTER
6

I woke up to the sound of a lawnmower running alongside the hotel. The sun was out and a light dry breeze pushed through the sheer curtain. A radiant humming was coming from the bathroom broken up by the faucet coming off and on. Sonya stepped out of the bathroom. The sleeves of her canary yellow blouse were rolled up and she had on cuffed blue jeans. A blue handkerchief held her hair back.

Her eyes looked amber in the light of the morning sun. "You're up. I was trying to clean the blood out of your shirt. How do you feel?" She knelt on the bed. I rubbed the side of my head and poked at the tight spot on my face.

"Better than fine, being here with you." I sat up and came to the realization I was only in my underwear. The sheet kept me covered at the waist. "I could use some food."

"Wonderful, you're hungry. That's a good sign, you know. The doctor called earlier and we went over everything one more time. Now what would you like?" Her smile shimmered and I pulled her close to me planting a kiss on unsuspecting lips. She reacted quickly, puckering up the second time and pressing back with equal pressure. Her neck bent and her head fell just out of my range, "You certainly are a quick healer. Now, how about something for that stomach of yours?" She stood up to make the call for our breakfast, not wanting the person on the other end to hear what might happen if she stayed in bed with me.

"Give me lots of eggs, lots of bacon and a strong pot of coffee." I said through a smile. She repeated the order through the line. Truth was my head felt like an axe was stuck behind my ear. My jaw ached like hell and it was murder to kiss her as I had. My hands were stiff and the skin over a couple of bruised knuckles was raw.

The food came and we sat at the small dinette, eating, sipping coffee and listening to the radio. With the shape I was in, Sonya had planned for us to stay in the room all day. The hotel manager called up to offer to wheel in a television for us to watch programs on. I was in too much pain to spend the day in bed so I suggested we head for the beach. It was only an hour drive. Sonya scrambled to toss things in a bag. She went on about how much fun we would have. I just smiled and chewed the last of the bacon.

Before we left, I phoned Lt. Blake. He mumbled in a low tone, letting me know there were others with him. I knew he couldn't speak, so I told him I was leaving town for the day and he could call me tonight at the hotel. He said it was best I leave, and then hung up. I wanted to cancel on Sonya right then and hurry down to the police station, interjecting myself into whatever Blake had cooking. Anxiety built in my chest as the case was rolled around in my aching head, when Sonya announced she was ready to go. Her beaming smile melted my heart and I forgot all about leaving her side.

[79]

After I swallowed a couple white pills from the doctor with what was left in the special brown bottle I brought, and was quickly feeling all right. We gassed up the International and hit the road for Daytona Beach.

Off A1A we parked in a sand dune. Our shoes were off and pant legs rolled up. We walked hand-in-hand along the lapping ocean. It was low tide and the water was flat - Lake Atlantic. A stiff breeze came off the dunes splattering our faces with salt and sand. I put my jacket over Sonya's shoulders. I picked a few seashells while she chased small tropical colored fish swimming in tight formation in the shallow water. A Willys-Overland Jeepster filled with teenagers raced by blowing its horn as the passengers waved. We waved back and walked some more until the sun started going down in the west. A hazy, yellow glow shimmered from the boardwalk just south of us. Faint music made it to our ears as a Ferris wheel went around and around.

The boardwalk had coquina rock walls with a concrete surface. A large coquina clock tower showed the time with a green grass lawn sprawled out in front. Jazz music carried over the water as a band kicked off at the casino at the end of the pier. We walked up and down and stopped to eat a couple of dogs and sip a beer. We sat and listened to the incoming tide. A man hollered out of the darkness near the lapping waves. His car was stuck in the sand and now the tide was pulling deeper. A cop blew his whistle and a few guys, bronze from their day in the sun, came to his rescue. A few heaves and hoes and the car budged.

We continued on to Main Street. We wandered around, window shopping. I admitted I was a little tired, so we took a cab a couple miles back to where we had parked the pickup.

"Is it time to go Cotton?" Sonya asked running her arm down the side of mine.

"Not just yet." I said reaching into the cab and pulled out a woven multi-colored Mexican blanket. We climbed into the bed of the truck, wrapped ourselves up and stared out at the stars. They were bright twinkling things; constellations of Greek heroes and gods. Sonya nuzzled her head into the crook of my neck. I felt her moist lips taste the sea salt on my neck. She moved her puckering lips up along my cheek then over to my own anticipating lips. I rolled half on top over her, my large frame blotting out her own. She reached up under my shirt and felt my bare skin, running her nails from my chest to my bellybutton. Her hot breath increased in repetition. My right hand slid up along her thigh, over her hip and to the top button of her shirt. I snapped the buttons one by one until the shirt fell open. I ran my hand over full twin mounds with pink nipple peaks. Her chest heaved. I could feel my heart pounding in my still split skull. It had been a long time, too long, since I treated a woman this way. I licked my lips tasting her chalky lipstick. She rolled to her left, rising above me. My back ached in the spots where I was pummeled the night before, but it was lost in the adrenaline pumping through me. She leaned in and we kissed some more.

After a few minutes of playing who's on top, Sonya sat up to catch her breath. She said playfully, "What is it about you Cotton that makes a woman lose her mind?" She pulled her shirt closed without buttoning it. I shrugged and dropped my head back against the rear cab window. In light of twinkling stars and a three quarter moon, Sonya's face grew cold. She dropped her chin into her chest. She made a little squeak as she sucked in a breath. I rubbed both her arms, asking what the matter was.

"What if you had died last night?" She refused to lift her head.

"Where is this coming from all of a sudden?" I tried a soothing voice, but it just sounded condescending.

"First Henry, then almost you." She picked her head up and squared her eyes on mine. "I hate that crummy town Cotton, I hate it." A balled up little fist bounced off my chest. I pulled her into me squeezing her so she would not hurt herself.

"Look at me. I'm not dead. I was before I met you, almost, that is. Always, half in a bottle and careless with my life, but you righted all that wrong. Honey, having you beside me has shown me how foolish I was. I haven't tied one on in three days - and look," I lifted a steady hand, palm down. "No shakes."

Warmth rushed over her cheeks as they pushed up under a great big toothy smile. Her balled up fists relaxed as she swung them around my neck. My steady hand reached up for a handful of chestnut curls.

"It's been a crazy couple of days," she continued, "Maybe we should head back to town."

I reluctantly agreed. With our shirts buttoned up, we drove out of the beach, heading back to Orlando and the Orange Court Hotel.

It was around eight when I swung the pickup in the semi-circle drive of the hotel. A skinny white kid in a white shirt and red jacket jogged out to meet us. I was already out, and had the door open for Sonya when he arrived.

"Park it close," I said. "And run the keys up to three-oh-eight. Got it?"

The kid nodded as he jumped behind the wheel. He had a little trouble getting the International out of first, but soon had it away and parked.

Sonya and I held hands, keeping our eyes locked on one another all the way back to the room. Once in the room, we rinsed the sand and salt from our faces. I pounced on the bed first. Sonya flipped the light out before she came out of the bathroom. Only grey moon light shown through the open window. It was enough light to catch on every curve and tip of her bare body. I suddenly felt overdressed and hurried out of my clothes. She stepped slowly to the edge of the bed.

"Don't make me regret this, Chamberlain Cotton" was all she said as she slipped between the sheets.

A ringing phone woke us both up. Sonya pulled a down pillow over her head as she rolled to the corner of the bed. I reached out and yanked the receiver, pressing it to my ear.

"Yeah."

"Cotton?" It was Lt. Blake. My eyes opened a little to see the time. It felt too early to be nine thirty. Blake went on, "I was with the mayor all day yesterday. We called the governor and went over everything we got on Jeffers. He wanted to get the FBI involved and leave it at that."

I butted in, "No way."

"Yeah, that's what I told him, to the disgust of the mayor. Shit, Cotton, this may have just cost me captain."

I cleared my throat. "Not when we bust this scum and Bobby writes you up as the hero. Put the FBI on Miami Trust. When we make our move here, there is bound to be chaos there." Sonya rustled beside me. I could feel her naked backside against my thigh.

"We really think alike, Cotton. In order for this to work, you and I need to stir the pot up here. How soon can you meet me here?" Excitement grew in the Lieutenant's voice.

"I'll be right over." I dropped the receiver. Sonya murmured something about it being too soon. I rolled her over and kissed her. She wrapped her arms around me and begged with her body for me to stay. My hand ran over her offer. I pulled away, telling her I'd make good when I got back. She pulled the sheet over her head.

I dressed in the bathroom to avoid temptation. In the mirror I could see the bruise was yellowing letting me know it was healing. I needed a shave bad, but skipped it. The cold water I splashed on my face would have to substitute for coffee until I got to the station.

Outside the air bit, another front had pushed through, dropping the temperature again and delaying the motor from heating. I had the heat blasting, having taken only my sport coat with me two nights ago. I thought of stopping off at my office, but was too eager to get to headquarters. Blake would have some black lambskin get-up, stinking of cop, for me to wear.

The streets were bare; a few shop owners were just unlocking doors and flipping closed signs to open. Neon lights blinked on, ushering in another shopping day before Christmas. There were only four left.

I had to circle headquarters twice before finding a spot to park. All three of the visitor spots were taken. This town needed a new police building. With both sets of Henry's books in my hand I ascended the short granite steps, taking two at a time. The cell doors must have just opened on the drunk tanks as a league of hobos and tom cats came spilling through the doors. I held the doors as they passed, my nostrils filling with the odor of sour lemons and bathtub gin. The morning sun poisoned their eyes like vampires who did not make it back to their coffins in time.

I hurried up a tile staircase with a well-polished wood baluster, and straight down a busy hall. Phones rang, typewriters chirped and someone was yelling. I walked through homicide against a few bitter stares. Cops - the law was theirs and theirs alone, no room for freelancers such as me. I grabbed the patina brass knob of Lieutenant Blake's office to find it locked. On the other side, a hand was quick to spin a key and the door parted a couple of inches. A face I didn't know stared back at me, his eyes filled with hurried anticipation for what I had to say. His hair was silver with waves of black left in it. His nose dipped low on his face, allowing long nose hairs to intermingle with his peppered mustache.

"I'm here to see Lieutenant Blake. Name's Chamberlain Cotton."

[85]

Blake's voice barked behind the silver-haired man. "Mr. Mayor, please let him in."

The mayor stepped back, pulling the door wide. I walked through, setting the pair of ledgers on Blake's desk and dropping my hat on top. The silver fox resumed his seat in a plush chair in the corner of the cramped office. A man stood from a chair across from Blake's desk. He was tall and lean, with short cropped hair. He held out his hand.

"Cotton," Blake said, "This is ADA Henderson. And, I believe you know the city mayor." I did not know the mayor, but I nodded anyway. The mayor returned the nod, crimping his lips together, acknowledging his own celebrity.

The assistant district attorney took a seat. I dragged a chair over from under a coat rack. Blake continued, "The governor was nice enough to appoint Mr. Henderson to Special Prosecutor. He's from outside the county. We don't know how deep this runs."

Blake brought me up to speed. They had been on it since five a.m., playing phone tag with the governor in Tallahassee. It was a strong accusation for a cop to call out another cop of racketeering and gross abuse of the badge. If one single step in this case were wrong, a single "t" left uncrossed, Blake, the ADA and the mayor would be disgraced, and probably out of a job. Calls were put into the FBI and they were still waiting to hear back. All they were told by the Feds was that the Coposey Crime Syndicate was still very active in Miami and that they had them under surveillance. They were in bed with a Cuban outfit in Miami. The Feds made it very clear we were not to go in guns blazing to take down Jeffers and any of the Coposey gang in operation in central Florida.

"I guess they take us for a bunch of hicks running wild among the groves." Blake shoved a pinch of chaw in his lower lip.

"And you wonder why I work alone." I smirked at Blake.

"Dagnabit Cotton, we got to work together on this."

"Mr. Cotton," said the ADA, breaking up the little family spat, "I understand this all started with a client of yours, Henry Clementine."

"You can call me Cotton. Mister is reserved for important people. Yeah, he was my client. He wanted me to check in on Jeffers. Henry knew something was wrong. He kept a second set of books." I handed the ledgers over to the ADA. He flipped through them while I recanted the adventures of the last forty-eight hours. "And then I woke up with a goose egg behind my ear and Blake acting worried for me." I bounced a grin over to Blake who returned it by spitting tobacco juice into a coke bottle, disgusting habit.

"That reminds me Cotton, I have a book of mug shots for you to flip through to try to identify either of the men that attacked you." Blake grabbed the phone and told the cop on the other end to send Arnie up with the book. He hung up and leaned back in a stiff wooden chair. Silence fell over the four of us. Outside, the room was a bustling police office with calls coming in and men with guns going out. We sat.

Finally, I asked, "Are we done here?"

[87]

"Yep.   You can wait out there for Arnie.   You remember him don'tcha? Tall, gangly fella."

"You can't be serious." I interrupted the lieutenant. "We need a plan to take Jeffers down and make sure the Coposey Syndicate isn't moving into Orange County." I balled my fist, bouncing it on the arm of my chair.

Blake's eyes went round.   He leaned forward and dribbled into his bottle.

The Mayor chimed in with a canned political tone, as if I was one of his constituents, "Mr. Cotton, what we have here will take some-"

Blake snapped, "And *we*, actual law enforcement, are taking care of it. This is going to take coordination with multiple agencies.   It's going to take planning and we have got to get it right or Clinton Jeffers and any other scum bag tied in on this walks. I know you, Cotton. I know the way you operate." Blake picked his stout frame out of the chair. "So I'm going to tell you right now, if I catch you sniffing around the Depot, Jeffers, or tangling with any out-of-towners, I'll throw you in the can and worry about the charges later."

I opened my clinched jaw to tell him, the ADA and the mayor to shove it, when Arnie showed at the door.   I bounced out of my chair and walked out. I must be going soft or getting slow. Blake and I never tangled; we came close a couple times, but never crossed that line. I was angry. I was the one thumped on the head. I was the one who lost a client to this mess, and I wanted at it. I wanted to burn the whole thing down and sweep away the ashes so no one would ever know any of it existed.

Arnie said hello and put down the book. Seeing red blinded my eyesight. I flipped a couple pages and mumbled something about the two guys not being in there. In my gut, I knew where they were and it wasn't fair. For the first time in days I really needed a drink.

I raced the International over to my office. I made double-time getting up the stairs and into my office.

The bottom left-hand drawer kept my back-up piece and I felt I was going to need it. I unlocked it and pulled the black snub-nosed .38 out with the ankle holster. I bent over in the chair and started to strap it to my leg.

The office door pushed open. I snapped up with the .38, pointing it at the gut of my visitor. Willimina did not blink. Her face, frozen in calm, continued to flow ice through her veins. With a grin, she sauntered over to my desk. Her curves were wrapped in a black knee length dress with a white piping along the shoulders and down the sides, accentuating her hips. The neckline dipped far south, showing a constellation of light brown freckles across the valley of her chest. Her hair was down and flowing in waves over her shoulders. The make-up was just right today.

"I hope that thing doesn't go off prematurely." She plopped one-half of her ass on the corner of my desk. I slipped it in the leather holster and rolled down my pant leg.

She stretched out her arm, planting four fingers and a thumb on the wood top. Her muscular legs crossed as she leaned back, giving me a full look at the body of an active girl. I was slow to take it all in; that kind of form deserves a thorough look.

"What are you drinking?" she asked.

"Not today." I wheeled back in the chair, putting some distance between us. I said, "I don't get you, Willimina. You are two halves of a coin. One minute you are helping growers extorted by dear ole dad, the next you are flashing cat eyes asking for a drink."

Her head tilted back and she let a low laugh out, like a cough. "You're one to talk, Cotton. I read the file my father has on you."

"How'd you manage that?"

"Careep is a dope. Before this case you were a drunk, carrying a P.I. ticket just in case. Somehow, Henry convinced you to look into my father. Is that what got you back on track?" She stopped for a moment. "I think it was definitely a Clementine, but not Henry."

"Just what is this about?" I was getting anxious. I wanted to toss her out on her fanny and get over to her pop's place to start asking some real questions.

"Nothing," Her eyes went soft. She was starting to scare the hell out of me. "I just like you is all." Her smile showed off little square teeth.

"I kinda got the idea you might have something going with Sam."

"He's alright. Before all this mess with the depot, Sam really carried some weight in this county with the growers. Nevertheless, it was all fluff. I like real men, Cotton." She moved to the couch, leaving a trail of sweet and spicy perfume. It tasted like money in my mouth. I watched her swing her hips, the same as she had back in the street moments after Henry was killed. A dozen men, probably powerful in their own way, had tried and failed to unravel that jumbled ball of twine, but she could never be straightened out. She sure made it tempting to try.

"Well, you got one for the next ten seconds, so make it good." I splashed some rye into a pair of glasses. They clinked together as I held them in one hand, making my way across the office towards the couch. I handed one off while remaining standing.

She took a swallow then licked her lips. "I think my father is in over his head. Two cars full of rough-looking men came to the depot today. I don't know what they wanted. My father sent me away. His driver, Dixon, dragged me off before I could make Daddy tell me what was going on." She looked down to her glass, swirled the liquor and swallowed it all.

"Good."

"What is that supposed to mean?" Her voice cracked.

"I was on my way over to the depot when you dropped in." I switched my glass for her empty. She nibbled at it and then held it in her lap with both hands. Sitting there worried about her father, she looked innocent and about twenty years younger, like a little child who was just told her cat had to be put down. I got suckered in and sat down next to her.

"Oh Cotton, I think it best you stay away from there." Her eyes puffed out, like she wanted to get the tears going. Her hand landed on my thigh. She leaned in close, looking up at me. Her lips parted just enough for me to see her tongue run along her top teeth. Sweat ran down my back. I felt the nerve twitch in my leg, and it wanted to bounce autonomously. I grabbed her hand in mine and she dove first, stretching her slender neck as her lips met mine.

Her breath was warm and fast as we broke for air. I pressed her soft body against mine, running my hand over every curve. She tasted expensive.

Then, just as the heat was building, it went off for me. I felt a deep freeze funnel through my core. I needed a drink to thaw my insides so I could keep going. Then the cold seeped into my brain. The craving for whiskey intensified. I pulled back.

Willimina looked at me with her big mahogany eyes half wrapped in their lids. Her mouth hung open for business. The craving was thick, but I fought back. The image of Sonya's warm smile subdued the rising beast. The way she looked up at me with curious wonderment every time I spoke, drove the whiskey from my mind taking the cold with it.

"This will never work." I said. It had been six months since I got close enough to kiss a girl and in the last two days, I had two girls throwing themselves at me. What mixed up luck I have.

"I don't understand, Cotton." For the first time I think I heard her actual voice, not the act she put on in the street or in the car with Sam. This girl had been playing an act for a long time, only she never heard the director yell cut until now.

"I got a girl. And besides, sooner or later I would show some kind of weakness for the booze. That's when you leave and move on to another strong fella, who likes your sharp edges and thinks he's tough enough to dull them." I stood up and brushed imagined filth off my suit.

Willimina sat blank-faced for a moment. She took a breath and looked at me with a frown, "That is a shame, Cotton. A girl like me loves a guy like you even more once he has figured her out." Her voice was high and stupid.

A red flashing light from the parking lot below ended any more parting words we had for each other. I looked out. Below was Lieutenant Blake's car. He stood with the door open, one leg propped on the floorboard and the radio cord stretched to its limits. My phone rang.

"Yeah." I said dragging the phone back to the window.

"Cotton, it's Blake."

"Stalking is against the law, Lieutenant."

He looked up at the building, guessing which window was mine. "I saw your truck was still here but I wasn't going up all them steps if you weren't home. Now get down here." I watched him slide back into his car.

"I had other plans Blake."

"Like hell you do. I think we have the same reservation. Now hurry it up." The line went dead. The operator got on, but I hung up without hearing what she had to say.

"Well I have my marching orders. I want you to stay away from the depot and your house too. I don't care where you go, just not anywhere your father might be." I reached in that lower desk drawer for a box of rounds and slipped them in a coat pocket.

"I understand. Be safe would ya, Cotton?" She got up, slowly straightening out her wrinkled dress and planted a slow wet kiss on my cheek. I started for the door when she said, "Do you mind if I stay here, just for a little bit, until I can figure some things out?"

I agreed and heard a police siren belch from outside.

Blake was sitting behind the wheel of his running squad car smiling at me when I jerked the door open and jumped in. "You gersh durn son of a gun, Cotton. I'm probably going to lose my pension over this. Then what will Judith do with me? Listen if anyone asks, I came out after you strictly to bring you back."

I grinned back, "You sure laid it on thick at headquarters. I wasn't sure if you meant all that BS or not - thought you went soft."

"I meant every word of it. But hell, I figure if I go with you, it makes for some kind of legit business." Blake reached up to column shifter. I stopped him.

"I think it would be best to take my truck. It's less cop-like."

Blake tongued at the wad stuck in his lip. He pulled a coke bottle he kept wedged between the worn seat cushions and spat. "Okay" he said, hopping out of the car. He popped the trunk and grabbed a bulky hand held two-way radio. He spit brown juice on the black top and said, "This is good for about two miles." He handed me the radio and pulled out a Remington pump action twelve-gage and some shells he dumped into his sport coat pocket.

We climbed into the cab of my pickup. Blake grumbled about me not having gun racks and questioned why I even drove the darn thing. We pulled away, with Blake forgetting his coke bottle spittoon. I made him toss the chew.

Wagner

CHAPTER
7

THE sky was colored un-polished silver, with blotches of white but no blue. There was a breeze high in the trees and a sporadic sprinkling of rain as we jogged along Orange Avenue, south toward the depot.

"Weather man, put out a hard freeze advisory." Blake said off-hand, making small talk.

"Great, more good news for the growers." We had never spent this much quiet time together before. Our previous conversations consisted of exchanging facts and details, never chit chat. I knew he was married to a "Judith", but I had never met the woman. The only thing he knew about me was on record somewhere.

It was four o'clock when we pulled up to the limestone road leading to Jeffers's Depot. The long lines were gone and all the trucks had left for the day. With tomorrow's weather report out, none would be returning for a few more days. I slowly crawled the International down the limestone road, keeping us covered in tall brush and pine trees. When we could see the top pinnacle of the depot, I pulled the truck off the road. The plan was to lay some eyes on the building before riding in "guns blazing", as the Federals all believed we would. I believed we would too, just not without knowing the odds.

Blake slung the shotgun over his shoulder and the binoculars around his neck, as if we were out turkey hunting. He was quick to put in another pinch of dip, looking relieved once the nicotine began to circulate in his blood. A random breeze picked up, and we used it to cover our swift steps to the edge of the brush line.

Lieutenant Blake looked out onto the depot, with his eyes peering through the binoculars. The field was roughly two hundred square yards and I could count with the naked eye the men walking along the dock. All the doors of the depot warehouse were shut. From our side, there were three black sedans - Jeffers' noticeably absent. I counted four men pacing along the dock, each one carrying a handgun. Blake called out some details, but it was not much more than I could see with my 20/20 vision. I let him have his fun.

"It will be dark in about an hour." Blake said, suggesting one of the plans I was already thinking.

I shook my head no, knowing he was thinking same thing I was. We had hungry appetites and wanted to feed on the syndicate scum trying to make their move in Central Florida. I cocked my head to the side, in the direction of the truck.

Once out of sight, I shared my plan. "Let's just ride up there. We can take those four men."

Blake spat, and then said, "Okay... then what do I do with this?" He tapped the shotgun with two fingers.

We rode up slow to the depot. Blake sat in the bed of the truck with the shotgun wrapped in a Mexican blanket. His hat was off, and he made like his head was hurt. For effect, we put a little transmission fluid on a rag.

I rolled down the window and hollered, "Come quick! We had another accident!" The four men refused to leave their post. Blake began to wail and kick the side of the bed in agony.

The truck stopped and I hopped out. The men leveled their guns at me and I threw up my hands. "Take it easy, I got another injured driver here." I went around to the bed of the truck and helped Blake out. He kept the wrapped shotgun down by his leg and began to hobble like it was a crutch. In the hue of the evening twilight, it was hard to make out what it was.

They began to shout, telling us to stay where we were. Two of the men turned out to be Italian and the other two Cuban, judging by accents. We moved side by side up the stairs. Blake continued to moan. My voice went shrill a couple times calling for a doctor. When the biggest guy there got within reach, Blake swung the blanket wrapped shotgun across the man's temple. He crumpled over, his eyes spinning like a compass near a magnet. I threw a punch at the medium ginny in a shiny suit. He fell back against the metal door of the depot. I was quick to get my pistol out. Blake racked a round in the shotgun. The other two men threw up their hands.

The dust settled and we lined them up against the wall. One of the Cubans began muttering in Spanish what I took for last rites. The men had real fear in their eyes. We didn't wear shiny badges, nor did we show up in shiny police cars. For all they knew, we were a rival gang taking them out. Sort of a Valentine's Day Massacre, only we really were the cops. Blake had two pair of cuffs. I didn't think to bring any, as I wasn't planning on taking prisoners.

I made two of the guys drag the big guy over to some piping running up the brick wall. Blake slid the cuffs through and we had them taken care of. The next two, we cuffed through the door handle on one of the rollup bay doors.

"You know who you're messing with bozo?" One of the ginnies found his balls after we cuffed him, realizing we weren't going to shoot him at that point.

"Yeah, kinda think we do." I said, passing him by to get to the door to the inside. He continued to shout threats. Blake marched back while I held the door. He raised the shotgun, wiggling his finger on the trigger. The hood quieted down. As Blake began to lower his weapon, one of the men made the mistake of making eye contact. Blake jabbed the butt into the man's face, shattering his nose. Blake could not hold back the smile. He spat juice and then wiped his mouth with his sleeve.

Inside the depot was dark and quiet. Black towering stacks of crates, divided into rows, looked like a cityscape during a black out. A lone light, from an office above, lead the way to the stairs. We did our best to take each steal step as if it were made of rotten wood. About four steps from the top, my eyes became level with the gangplank. A line of office doors were to my left. I counted doors until I got to the one I remembered was Jeffers's office. The light was on, casting shadows of men moving about. I readjusted my grip on the pistol, becoming aware of its weight and balance. The hammer was back and I was ready to play.

We crawled low, just below the height of each office window. When we got to Jeffers's office door, Blake came around me to the other side. In the dim light, I could see the white's of Blake's eyes, his pupils enlarged, blocking out most of the grey of the iris. A low humming of voices came from under the door. Gradually the humming grew louder until distinguishable words were heard. I wanted Clinton Jeffers alive so I could kill him myself. It was time to get in there.

I reached up to the knob and twisted. The bolt came back as I held the knob turned so there would be no 'click'. I peeped through the crack. Careep sat at his desk, holding the side of his face with a blood soaked rag. His eyes opened wide and still. In less than a second, I froze and the one thought of being spotted rattled around my empty head, like dropping a penny in a jug. He didn't move. I didn't move except to blink.

I stood up and let myself in. Careep slowly rolled his eyes my way. He sat in silence staring at me. His face was drawn and grey. Someone hit him pretty hard, and he was just now coming to.

The front office was empty except Careep. Voices continued to heat up from inside Jeffers's main office. Blake came in behind me. Careep sat with one hand on the desk, his chair pulled up tight, and the other soaking blood in a rag. He did not say a word as we passed him.

Blake and I squared at the door. In silence we negotiated the plan, I would kick in the door and he would rush in first with the shotgun. The idea was for the show of force to restrain any careless thinking. On three, we went.

There was a moment of chaos as shouting came in three different languages. Jeffers sat behind his desk much as Careep did: hands out, pinned close to the tabletop. His face was spread wide in shock, his jaw open, making no sound. On either side of Jeffers, pointing handguns at Blake and me were the two dumb thugs that rolled me. I couldn't help but smile through all the shouting. The shouting continued a few moments longer. The thug to my right, with the nickel-plated .45, raised his empty left hand to try to level off the shouting.

"Whoa, whoa, whoa. Take it easy copper. We can cooperate." Vinny put the handgun on the desk and stepped back. The Cuban had more fire in his eyes. His gun was a lower caliber, probably responsible for Careep in the other room. The small barrel fanned at me, then Blake. Sweat bubbled on his brow.

Blake said, "You really want to shoot a cop, you dumb son of a bitch?" Then he jabbed the shotgun at him. Raulo complied, putting the gun down. Blake swooped up both pieces with one hand, holding the shotgun at belly level with the other. "Now get over there," Blake added, lining to two against the wall.

Raulo was dressed in a black, loosely woven, cotton shirt, unbuttoned at the top with a white undershirt beneath. He wore a white tightly meshed straw hat, with a black band around it. On his face, he had a black goatee. His lip curled at the corner and he muttered something in Spanish.

Vinny, the Coposey thug was dressed in a reflective steal blue suit with a purple tie and handkerchief in the pocket. He was a real gangster, all right, with well-polished nails and diamond pinky ring. He looked like he told his tailor to watch every bad detective movie in the last twenty years for inspiration.

Clinton Jeffers remained behind his desk. He gobbled the first couple words from his mouth then stood up. He wobbled, and then decided to sit back down.

"What're your names?" Blake commanded of the two thugs.

I piped in, "Raulo and Vinny, the two dirt bags that sapped me." Images of revenge filled my mind's eye. I wanted to pull the trigger right there and end both their miserable lives. I wanted to stand over their dying bodies as blood gurgled from their open mouths. I wanted them to see victory on my face, as their eyes rolled back in their dense skulls. Damn Blake for being here right now.

Clinton Jeffers finally came around. He spread his arms out across his desk and laid them carefully down as if spreading a sheet over his desk. "Now gentlemen, please, let's put the weapons away." His tone dripped in condescension. I suppose it is the only way he knew how to speak.

"Can it Jeffers! I'm the one with the badge!" Blake used the shotgun to guide Vinny over to where Raulo was standing near Jeffers and the ornate desk. I holstered my pistol, if nothing more than with the hope of luring one of the thugs to make a move.

"Now, I want some answers - starting with you two." The shotgun became an extension of Blake's arm, pointing at each man he spoke to.

"No Ingles." Raulo shrugged.

"Yeah what he said." Vinny hiked a thumb in Raulo's direction. Blake ran his free hand over his face, tugging on his chin.

"Okay, so you don't want to talk here. Well, we can take you down to the station. I can book you on carrying a gun. Just one-on-one in a room with no windows. Yeah, I'll get what I want out of you, 'Angless' or no 'Angless'." Blake motioned for the door.

Jeffers' eyes came off the desk. He was, for the moment, an actor on a stage. "Now just a minute, inspector. These men are on private property and are guests of mine. I will not be pressing charges." Pain circulated in his gut as the lie whispered from his lips. His head bowed to his left.

Curses rumbled from Blake's lips. To make matters worse, in the distance multiple sirens penetrated the steel walls of the depot, growing louder as the seconds ticked by. Anger welled up inside me; I knew where this story was headed. Blake had the two men that cracked my skull and Jeffers was not going to press charges. At most, they would be held on carrying guns and when the high price lawyers from Miami showed up, they would walk with sick grins on their ugly faces. I did not want to go back and face Sonya.

We stood there in the moments before the sheriff arrived. Blake spent the time trying to convince Jeffers of how foolish he was and that he had enough to lock these thugs up. Jeffers would hear nothing of it. I wanted to strike out. Punching the wall or pounding on Jeffers's desk to ease the acid running through my muscles. The sirens grew louder. My palms began to sweat. Each second the sirens sounded closer, I did not want to leave without killing someone. It was best to keep my distance.

As I walked out, Raulo locked onto me. He said, "Adios," and puckered his lips sending out a kiss. The hair on the back of my neck stood up. I balled a fist so tight it could have punched through steel. My head was not turned all the way, before Blake snatched me by the arm. He grunted for me to keep walking, and then shoved me toward the door.

I got out the door of the depot to find two county prowl cars, each with a red light doing circles on the roof. Two men in khaki uniforms, short black ties and six-pointed hats, fussed with cuffs on the gang members. I lit a cigarette in an exaggerated style making a racket with the Zippo. I blew out a long stream of white puff. I watched it divide in two and circle in on itself. A third sheriff slammed the trunk on one of the two cars.

Sheriff James Jameson stood holding a chrome flashlight a foot long. He was in the same khaki county uniform but lacked a tie. His hat was a dark brown, beaver skin Stetson and he had snakeskin hide over his boots. Wrapped around him was a brown jacket with a black fur collar around his neck. His holster was tanned leather and hung low on his thigh. He was character from a western in his own mind.

He was dressed every bit like a cracker sheriff, until he opened his mouth, "Well, nah who do we have here?" He was a Florida native all right, by way of Bean town. The Boston accent was heavy, leaving out every 'R'. His walk was pinned at the thighs, giving him a wobble as he moved. He kept the flashlight tapping in his palm.

"I'm here on official business with O.P.D." I flashed him my private investigator's badge. James's smile pushed the limits of the corners of his mouth. He pointed the well-worn chrome flashlight at me. I could see the bell was dented and the copper was pushing through a worn spot in the chrome.

"This here is unincorporated county, boy. City limits are *back thah* a couple miles." He was a foot from my face now. I blew smoke at him. The smile dipped fast and so did the hand holding the flashlight. Sheriff JJ socked me in the gut. I pushed out all the smoke left in me as I crumpled over. From the ground, I counted the scales on his snakeskin boots. This guy was a snake with a badge. One way or another, I was going to take that badge from him.

Blake came out with Raulo and Vinny behind a shotgun just as I was picking myself up off the concrete dock. Clinton Jeffers stumbled out of the depot close behind the trio. I could see Blake mouth a few dirty swears when he lowered the scattergun. "Howdy, Sheriff." He said through a forced grin.

"Lieutenant Blake, I said I was not pressing charges on...on these men." The spark in Jeffers's eyes went out once he saw Sheriff JJ standing near me. Unspoken words exchanged through eye contact between the two most powerful men in Orange County. Jeffers neared Blake, putting up a puckered hand on Blake's arm. In a near whisper he said, "Lieutenant, please let these men go before there is trouble."

Blake's eyes peeled back and the whites became consumed in fire. Through the years, I have known Blake to be an easy going, cool tempered man. That all changed when a criminal ordered him to release other criminals. With his right hand, he snatched the old man by the shoulder. His lips disappeared into the corners of his mouth, as tobacco stained teeth flashed. "Who do you think you are Clinton Jeffers, that you can tell me to release a prisoner?"

JJ called out, "Lay off Blake. This isn't your jurisdiction." His words fell on deaf ears as Blake continued to squeeze Jeffers's arm. The old man trembled as blood evacuated from his face. The once virile old man knew he had gone too far.

"Blake!" Sheriff JJ called out drawing his side iron. The other two deputies hesitated then drew their pistols as well. My head went into an electrical storm, trying to force my numb hands into action. My gut overruled it, keeping my body still.

Blake dropped the old man, whispering "I'm coming for you, Jeffers." Blake turned to JJ with the same heated disposition.

"Now, Blake, I could take you in for that, but I hate paper work, so why don't you take your hired gun and beat it before I change my mind?" Sheriff JJ left the pistol leveled on Blake as he swung the shotgun over his shoulder. The lieutenant kept his eyes straight ahead towards my truck as we retreated. Blake and I exchanged no words on the hike back. There was nothing to say. We both knew what we were getting ourselves into.

Half-way back to town I finally broke the silence, "We tipped our hand. It was my fault, Blake." Blake stared off a thousand yards ahead.

"Yep." The fire was smoldering still. He would not let this rest. I could not tell who he was madder at, me or the barrel Jeffers and the sheriff had us over.

"They'll probably lay low for a while, let things cool off." I was angry too, but knew that I could let things cool off, and then do what I do best and keep outside the law to do my work. I needed to let Blake cool it, too, so he would stay off me the next few days.

"No. They will go full-steam ahead knowing full well there is nothing we can do about it." He mumbled some more swear words then looked my way. "I should have known better Cotton. It wasn't all your fault, you don't have city and county limits. You can go anywhere in the state with that badge and do your work, I can't."

We rode along in silence the rest of the way.

I pulled the pickup near Blake's squad car. He got out. I stayed behind the wheel.

"Cotton," he said in low and soft tones, holding the door open, "They have guns backed up by their badges. No matter how tarnished the brass is, it's still the law. We need to do it by the book, and with overwhelming numbers."

I responded with a nod. Truth was, we both had a lot of work to do and, from here on out, it would have to be separate and each in our own way. Blake would go back, catch hell from the mayor and ADA, then get to work on getting warrants. I was going to go my own direction, just as I always had. Blake was right about me and my limits. The Coposey Syndicate would move without fear in the county, their pay-rolled Sheriff at their side. Embolden confidence would bring their guard down, and I would be there waiting for them.   Then every bit of my killing would be justified.

CHAPTER
8

I zipped the ole International up Orange Ave and dropped into the Orange Court Hotel. The same bellman as before was there to catch my keys as I let them fly. He asked if I wanted it nearby and running. I told him not tonight. Tonight I was headed for one place and not leaving until day light.

"Mr. Cotton." The voice came from behind the lobby desk, catching me off guard. I spun on my heels just before getting on the elevator. "Oh, Mr. Cotton, a word please..." It was Jon, the front desk manager. He had a smug, know-it-all look on his face. After the day I'd had, I wanted to slap it right off.

"Yeah?" was my response. I did not give him the satisfaction of caring what he had to say.

Jon cleared his throat, "Miss Clementine is in the Diner."

Across the lobby hung a pair of doors with six panes of glass on each of them and large polished brass handles. A neon sign above simply stated *Diner*. I made my way for the doors. As I passed the front desk, Jon leaned his round body too far over the desk, nearly tipping over the side. His face strained red, "Mr. Cotton, the Orange Court is a family establishment. I must insist all guests sign in." His face grew long and pointed.

I pulled my coat apart by placing my hands on my hips. The hog leg of my .45 poked out from under my arm. Jon's eyes zeroed in on it. "Is that so?" I asked. "Well, not this time." I started for the door once more.

"But I must insist, Mr. Cotton, or I will be forced-"

"I must insist you keep your little fat nose out of it!" I moved in inches from his face until I could feel his quick, scared breath on my face. My jaws clenched as I let my lips form all the words, "In fact I insist you keep quiet about Miss Clementine and I staying here. Unless Lieutenant Blake from OPD calls himself - you never heard of us. Understood?"

He slithered back to his side of the counter. I buttoned my coat and went to find Sonya.

The joint was clean and smelled of hot cooking oil and whipped cream. Christmas songs played quietly on the jukebox, reminding me I did not have a tree up yet. The booths were wrapped in red leather and six-inch wide panes of frosted glass separated them. I had to walk by each table until I spotted Sonya, wearing an adorable grin. Before her, on the table, was a book split open and next to that, a half-slurped float. I took off my hat and sat down across from her.

"I was getting worried about you." Sonya's red lips parted slightly. I could tell she wanted to say more, but stopped herself.

"You don't have to do that."

She frowned. She liked worrying about me. It was her way of showing me she cared. "Well okay. Maybe you can a little." I said with a grin. Her hand reached out across the table and grabbed my wrist. I put my other hand on top of hers. We got lost in each other's eyes for a moment. The waitress came over and broke up the staring contest.

The name on the badge said Flo. She was in her early forties, with an outdated hairdo. She had lipstick on her teeth and multiple stains on her white apron. "What can I getcha?" Another Yankee transplant.

"Cheeseburger - medium, and a coke." I did not bother with a menu, places like this were good for one kind of plate, and I just ordered it. Flo scribbled it down and looked at Sonya.

"I'll just have a side of fries." She smiled, but did not get one in return. The rudeness went without comment as Flo left to put in our orders.

"Not hungry?" I leaned over the table and sipped on the melted shake.

"I've been picking all day." Sonya closed the book. It was a crime novel she picked up from the hotel store. I looked at the cover art. A half-naked woman sat on a bed, clutching a sheet. From the corner, a hand held a gun with the hammer cocked. Her eyes looked angry more than they did frightened. Real tough broad, I guess.

"What are you reading?" Sonya put a flat palm over the cover of the book. Blood filled her cheeks and her eyes looked away.

"Nothing." She said sheepishly, sliding the book under the table.

"I don't know. Looks pretty good." I tried not to smile too big.

"Oh, stop it. I've been bored and-"

"Do you usually read detective books?" I reached under the table and grabbed at the book. She pulled it away, so I grabbed her knee. She let out a squeal and the whole diner looked over. We laughed and she tossed the book at me.

I flipped the pages and read off the back cover. "This Taver Mcgullan sounds like a real tough mug. Hate to run into him in a dark alley."

"Stop making fun." Her eyes got sore. "I was just doing some research is all."

"Real detective work is never like this." The waitress set down my coke and walked off. I plucked a straw from the glass container on the table and slurped it down.

"How is the case going?" Her eyes lost the innocence of moments before.

I could not keep the big wall of Sheriff James Jamison from her. She deserved to know. I looked down at my hands and picked at a callus in one of my palms. "There's a few obstacles in the way, but I'll get Jeffers and those responsible." I looked up at her big brown eyes. They were like glass now, filled to the brim with tears that had not yet fallen. "I made a promise to your brother and to you. Don't worry."

Sonya stifled a sniffle. With her left hand, she pulled the sleeve of her right and blotted her eyes. Flo showed up with our food. I was not hungry anymore. All I wanted to do was get back out in the cold and hunt a killer, or killers. I wanted to pump lead into the bastards that destroyed a girl's family and hid behind the law to do it. Filthy dirty cops were going to burn with the rest of the trash.

The plates before us were steaming fresh, but we were not hungry. I took a couple bites, small ones, of the burger and Sonya dipped the same fry three times in ketchup before eating it. We both tried to say something, but the words trailed off before we ever completed them. Tonight was supposed to be fun. With the help of Blake, we were going to take down Jeffers and kick the Coposey Syndicate out of central Florida. That did not happen. It ended, facing a bigger wall in Sheriff JJ and his two hired gun deputies. The guilty went free tonight and it was eating at my insides.

"I'm sorry, Sonya," I said extending out my hand across the table for hers. "Today should have ended differently and it's just not sitting right with me. I'm afraid I won't be much company tonight." Her slender fingers gripped my hand tight. It relaxed and was withdrawn.

She forced a smile through a frown and ended up breaking even. "I know, Cotton." She leaned in and lowered her voice, "We had such a good time the other night," She said in a half- whisper, looking around the diner. "I just didn't want it to end." Sonya leaned back and folded her hands in her lap.

"Listen kid, it's not over. I just need to do what I swore I would." I slid out of the booth. I tossed a fin on the table. Leaning into Sonya, I said, "I don't let go of things easy, this case - or you." She looked up at me and wrapped her hands around my neck. I almost jerked her out of the booth. Three quick pecks across my face left me feeling flushed. She let go and settled back into the booth.

[113]

"Now, just you hang tight, okay?" I put my hat on and headed for the door. I left her there, with a big grin across her pretty little face. It felt good to make someone else happy for a change. The only comfort I'd had in six months was the time I'd spent in a bottle. Any little pleasure I managed from being drunk was gone the second I woke up out of it. This was different. This feeling was something that wouldn't leave me in the morning and would keep me warm each night I went to bed. I was happy, but not dumb. Those warm feelings would have to come after I took care of Jeffers and the Coposey Syndicate, even if I had to kill each and every one of them. Sheriff JJ would have to be handled by Blake and the ADA. Those deputies would have me full of lead and six feet under, before any inquisition could clear my name.

I went out through the double doors of the lobby. A flash of arctic air slapped my face. I licked my lips to keep them from cracking apart. Just in the time I spent with Sonya, the temperature dropped a dozen degrees. These twenty degree swings in high temperatures were gonna make us all sick. The bellman was quick with my truck. The motor was still warm from driving in, and the heater was working hard. The cab felt cozy as I cut left out of the hotel and cruised south down Orange.

All the Christmas decorations were in full illumination. Strung across the street every block or so was another symbol of the season, lit up in greens, reds and whites. I took it slow, allowing the season make an impression on me. I wished Sonya was by my side, commenting on the colors and arrangements. There would be next year and the one after that.

I pulled into the parking lot adjacent my building. Out of habit, I glanced up at my office window. The light was on. My rational mind told me it didn't mean much - not too unlike me to leave the light on, but my body was reacting totally different. My eyelids pulled tight at the corners and I felt for the grip of my pistol tucked under my coat. The weight was right, fully loaded.

I took the stairs to my floor. The hall door opened slowly, and I peered out down the long hallway to my office. The office door was open an inch, allowing a beam of forty watt light to cut the dark hall in half. I pushed my hat back on my head allowing in all the light my steel eyes could capture. My steps were light as I crept down, along with the .45 leveled out before me. Just outside my office, I paused for sound. Nothing.

I slipped out of my overcoat along with the hat. I wanted to be loose for whatever was inside.

With my left hand, I pushed the door open and fanned the pistol left to right. My eyes went to the black mass lumped on the floor. I could not make out a face, but, whoever it was he was out. I peered into the cell and confirmed it was empty. My office was trashed. All my desk drawers were out of the desk and tossed about the room. The cushions were off my sofa and my three-drawer filling cabinet was on its side. The room smelled heavy of spiced cologne, a smell that was becoming too familiar with my senses. I went back to the unconscious mass on my torn-apart office floor.

I rolled it over. Her face had a deep red rash across the left side and her lip was split and two sizes bigger than I remembered. All of her limbs and digits were there. Willimina Jeffers looked to be in rough shape, but she would live. I cupped her jaw and gently shook her head. Her eyes came open and she blinked slowly. Her first words caught in a dry throat. I told her to relax and not speak, just nod. She agreed with a nod up and down.

"Can you move?"

She nodded yes and together we rose. I did most of the heavy lifting to get her to the couch. She laid back and pressed a palm against the side of her swollen face. Her brow crinkled and her mouth came apart. A little spit rolled down onto her black dress and silent sobs jerked her body about. I went to the floor beside my desk and grabbed a bottle of whiskey and a glass.

"Sip this." I said, and she put it to her busted lips. A little flinch came as the gold liquid touched the open wound.

"How bad is the pain? Do I need to call a doctor?" She swung her head 'no' and sipped again. I relaxed a little, knowing she would survive.

I looked around at the mess in my office. Forty-five rounds lay scattered about with old files on closed cases. My suits were on the floor and two drawers on the metal cabinet were open. The bottom one I kept locked. I inspected the deep scratches and dents around the lock. The lock had held. I made a note to send the manufacture a letter complimenting their craftsmanship.

The office was chilled, so I grabbed a blanket from the floor (where everything I owned was at the moment) and wrapped it around Willimina. I went out to the hall to retrieve my coat and hat and came back and sat beside her.

"Not going to ask who dun it?" she forced the words out with a half-grin, conscious of the split lip. I smiled back.

"I'm a detective, remember? Do you know how long you were out?"

She shook her head "no". I checked the time on my wristwatch. It was a quarter after seven.

"Can you walk me through it?"

She cleared her throat thoroughly before her monolog. "After you left, I sent Dixon away, telling him I wanted to walk around and Christmas shop for awhile."

"Dixon?" I broke in.

"The driver." She said in a manner of fact. "But I stayed here. Truth was I was too worried about you running off to the depot. I was convinced you would get hurt or worse." Her eyelids fluttered as she looked up at me from the corner. Skinny fingers crawled out from under the blanket and found the meat of my thigh.

"Cut it out." I swatted the curious fingers away. "We went over this." I got up and poured us both a drink.

"Anyway," she took the rejection well, jumping back in the facts, leaving out the cutesy talk. "I was here maybe an hour, I'm not sure exactly. I fell asleep. A knock on the door woke me. I opened it and four men in glitzy suits barged in. Before I could protest, I was swatted down. I never got up off the floor. One of them, kinda short and with a Spanish accent, bent over me and...and..." this time the tears rolled down. It was convincing, but I reserved final judgment.

[117]

Her forearm came up over her head and she burrowed into my shoulder. I remained still - this doll had proved loony before.

"Recognize any of them?"

The sobbing relaxed. She pulled back, fully composed. "It was them - the new business partners my father brought into town."

"What'd they want and what'd you tell them?"

Willimina recoiled back bringing her arm across her chest. "You're a cold one, Mr. Cotton." She hissed.

"Only on the inside. What'd they want?" I kept level.

Her eyes scanned me over looking for a tell. There was none. "To deliver a message. The little guy said you and your cop friend are dead men. Then, he hit me and I went unconscious." She gingerly touched at her wounds.

I got off the couch and went to the toppled over cabinet. I pulled a ring of keys and fit one into the lock. The drawer rolled out and the contents spilled to the floor. A Thompson with four clips came out. The clips were attached two together, facing in opposite directions, so when I emptied one clip I could just flip it and reload without having to dig out another one. The clips were empty. I pulled a green canvas satchel full of loose thirty caliber rounds and sat down at my desk. Laying everything out on the desk, I began slipping round after round into the black clips.

Each round that slipped into the clip was expected to do a job, a big job. Something began to claw its way up from deep in my gut. I worked like a machine on an assembly line sliding round after round into clip after clip. My mind was fixated on one thing - killing. The *live and let live* attitude I carried as a drunk was replaced with a *kill and kill some more* attitude.

Two minutes of silence later, Willimina said, "Got a cigarette?", as she slipped over to the desk. With both hands planted, she leaned forward so I could see down her V neck dress to her belly button. I took in the show then reached in my left inside coat pocket and pulled out a deck of smokes. I tossed it to her and went back to loading. She lit one, exhaling smoke around me. "You gonna get 'em all, Cotton?" Smoke leaked out of her nostrils.

"Every last one." I had had my fill. Gangsters from down south are piling up in my town and threatening my life because I do my job. A few days ago, I would've been half-drunk, my chin bobbing a few inches above a bar, with the rest of the bar flies drowning out memories of things we cannot fix. Regret is the great de-motivator. However, that was then. Boy, did these thugs have bad luck. I was sober with something to fight for. With every steel jacketed round I slipped into the clip, I pictured it charging out of the barrel hot, spinning until it collided with one of these shiny suit bozos, splitting their flesh and taking their life.

My lips pulled tight in a grin as Willimina wished me luck and made for the door. She paused there for a moment, holding onto the door but I was not interested. My mind stayed focused on the process of killing. A rough idea of heading down to the depot and just randomly shooting was quickly tossed. After the day's foul up, a contingency plan for my return would have to be in place for them. I had to keep this fire stoked, but make sure it burned all through the night.

All the weapons were loaded, checked and rechecked. I switched out my loafers for a pair of boots, and a pair of denim for my wool pleated pants. With the freeze warning out, I left wearing a black and red plaid jacket.

The International sat idling, getting warm as I sat thinking. Going in guns blazing might be the fun I was looking for, but it was stupid and I wasn't stupid. Whenever things got moving too fast, I would have to pause and step back. All the facts added up nicely: *A rich man gets greedy and starts to extort the very men who made him rich. When there is resistance, he calls in some muscle from down south. Well, the muscle is too big for the old man and he is suddenly in over his head.* Sure, it added up, but what happened when I started to divide the total sum number? I got a fraction, not a whole number. That tells me I'm looking for the common denominator in all of this.

With the missing denominator out there, I flipped on the headlights, ready to take off. My eyes peeled back as a man in a cafe skin jacket tossed up his arms. I quickly recognized that pale yellow face. I rolled the window down.

"You almost got dead reporter." I let off the brake and the truck rolled a couple feet, as Bobby came around my window.

"I was almost killed by fright. I couldn't see you in the cab. You scared the hell out of me, Cotton." Bobby jammed his hands into wool-lined pockets. "Can I get in?"

I nodded and Bobby jogged around to the passenger's side. He hopped in, bringing the bite of the frosty air with him.

"What's up, chum?" I said, wanting a smoke but not wanting to crack a window, even an inch. Bobby looked down at my Thompson resting near my leg. He shook his head with a light hearted "no".

"Glad I found you in time. I kept digging into those reported accidents and claims at Miami Trust." His voice found an excited level, "Those injuries were bogus. Half the time the drivers were not even there. The Depot puts in a phony claim, an adjuster signs off and money is paid out."

"To who?"

"Supposedly the drivers. They're a tight lipped bunch and everyone around the depot is real jumpy these days with the mob presence. I was making phone calls all day and -"

"Foot notes Bobby." He was going off in a direction I could care less about.

"Sorry. I finally got one driver to open up. An Earl...Earl somebody. I have it written down. Anyway, he didn't know anything about it. He said he hasn't had an accident in four years and never missed a day of work." Bobby's face was all smiles, lit up in green and red Christmas lights shining in from the street.

"So the depot is washing more than just fruit these days."

"I knew it had to be more than just racketeering."

"You got a good nose, Bobby. Listen, I need you to get in touch with Blake and fill him in on what you know in case they haven't got this far - and I doubt they have."

"Sure thing, Cotton." Bobby's smile slid into a frown when he looked once more at the Thompson, "What exactly are you going to do?"

"That's just for just in case. Now that we really have some dirt on these scumbags, I need you to watch your back. I suggest getting down to the police station right away and hanging there until these guys are gone." I reached down to my boot and pulled my snub-nosed thirty-eight. I handed it to him, butt first. Bobby was slow to grab a hold of it.

His head shook, disapproving of my safety advice. "I'm a reporter not a gunfighter." As if on cue, a pair of head lights shined bright in my rearview mirror, illuminating the cab and squinting our eyes. Our heads turned in unison behind us. Through the shining lamps, I made out the doors of a sedan opening. I barked out for Bobby to get down.

A pair of automatics sounded off as I popped the clutch and jammed the skinny peddle down. The truck jumped forward went about thirty feet and T-boned into a parked car. My shoulder hit the steering wheel as Bobby slipped to the floor. Bullets punctured steel walls and shattered the glass of the cab. The Thompson had fallen to the floor and slid under the seat. I folded in half on the bench while Bobby as balled on the floor. He was up before I was squeezing the trigger of the thirty-eight. Three shots pierced my eardrums. One headlamp went out. The onslaught paused for a moment as the shooters took cover.

It was enough time for me to grab the Thompson and roll out the driver's side door. I popped up near the bed of the truck and fired off a dozen rounds from the Thompson.

The gangster's car sparkled like a fourth of July night sky. Shadows took cover behind heavy objects. I shot out the other headlamp to level the playing field.

A black mass cracked off a shot and, in the muzzle flash, I saw a face. My trigger finger jerked, releasing a four round burst from the Thompson. He got off a second shot but his gun hand was raised up overhead as his body toppled back. A valley of fire lit up the darkened parking lot. I kept my head low, bringing up the Thompson over the bed of the pickup. I returned fire until the clip emptied.

Bobby snaked his way around a few parked cars, going unnoticed by the thugs. He popped up at my eleven o'clock to fire off two more shots. One connected with a black mass. The mass slumped to one side and let out a holler. The thug behind the passenger door slid across the seat behind the wheel. He fired the sedan and backed out, screeching the tires all the way out of the parking lot. Once in the street he tried to K turn, forcing a lone motorist up a curb. I flipped the clip in the Thompson while on the move.

The street provided better lighting and I found my target with ease. Shooting a Thompson did not take much skill. And even less when you are trying to expel every round of the thirty in the clip. I sprayed lead hard and fast.

The driver threw the car in drive and hammered once again on the accelerator. The tires chirped and the RPM's red-lined. He jerked the wheel, zigzagging the car. It was useless against the hot lead I laid down. The motor went to an idle and the car coasted into a parked car along the street. I waited for him to come out, but he did not stir.

With Bobby behind me, we approached the sedan. All the windows were blown out and the street lamp illuminated the fresh torn steel against the black body of the sedan at every bullet entry. I had my forty-five out now, cocked and pointed at the car.

A garbled whimper came from the back seat. I peaked over the rear door. A man in a black trench coat lay holding his left arm. His teeth clenched tight as sweat poured from his brow. Up his neck and on his face were freckles of maroon goop.

"Got a live one," I said over my shoulder. Sirens bellowed in the distance. There was no need to call in the police.

Convinced the bleeding man was unarmed and the driver was dead, I asked Bobby how he was doing. Any trace of Spanish blood was gone from his face, now pale and gaunt. Steaming breath rapidly expelled from his open jaw. His eyes were fixed on the bleeding man I pulled from the car.

"Whoa." His voice was forced and rattled. "That was…it happened pretty fast." His hand was shaking when he handed over the pistol. The crooked grin assured me it was not fear shaking Bobby; he was coming down from the adrenaline. I did not want to admit I was a little excited too.

I knelt beside the bleeding thug and grabbed his mangled arm. He let out a yelp.

"Your hit squad failed." I grumbled through a tight jaw. "Who was next?" He did not say anything, so I squeezed his arm once more. The sirens were closing in. He knew help was on its way. The cops would patch him up nice and feed him soup, then maybe in a day or two ask him some questions. I needed answers now. Blake's and Sonya's lives depended on it.

I pressed my pistol barrel against his chest. "If you won't talk, you're no good to me alive." I thumbed the hammer back. The thug looked to Bobby for help. The reporter remained still.

"There was just us." He forced out the words through heavy breath. I clenched down like a vice on his arm. I could feel the bones beneath my fingers as blood bubbled to the surface of the wound. "I swear!" He shouted, his body stiffening like I had just jolted him with electricity. I was satisfied.

Once again, a couple of uniformed cops disarmed me. I called for them to get Lieutenant Blake on the phone - that it was a matter of life or death. The pair shouted me down and took their sweet time examining my private investigators ticket and my gun permit. I looked up at the black windows becoming yellow with artificial light. Dozens of faces pressed against the glass from the buildings surrounding the parking lot. An ambulance arrived to take the one thug away. I tried once more to question him, but the uniforms forced me away. They had their own questions. Separately they questioned Bobby and me. When our stories matched, they dialed back on the tough cop routines.

Another uniform came over from examining what was left of my pickup. He told one of the other uniforms that Blake was on his way. I relaxed a little, knowing they had contact with him.

Lieutenant Blake arrived forty-five minutes later. His eyes were tired and he wasn't wearing a dress shirt under his coat.

Blake ran a meaty paw over three days of stubble, "I haven't been to bed in two days, Cotton! Two days! While you rested it up in a hotel, room service and pretty eyes playing nursemaid, I was working on this case. I finally got home tonight, climbed into a warm bed next to Judith, closed my eyes and the phone rings and rings and rings." His head swiveled back and forth I thought it would roll right off his shoulders.

"Now's not the time to sleep, Blake. We need to-"

Blake cut in, "I sit up to answer the phone, and see a red flashing light outside my house. Two plain-clothes guys are standing with guns drawn on a sedan full of thugs with guns. You know how mad that makes me, Cotton?" The corners of his mouth pulled down and purple veins rose to the surface of his ruddy skin. His right hand balled so tight, I expected blood to seep from the grooves.

I smiled. "Thanks for the heads up." I slapped him on the shoulder.

Blake glared back then his face softened. "Ah, nuts. It was the ADA's idea. I didn't even know he put the guys on my house. He said he's dealt with the Coposey Syndicate before and did not want to take any chances."

"Back to business then?" I said. Blake nodded. I added, "We need to strike while they think they are safe.

Raulo believes I've just been taken out. They are making their power plays right now."

"Lieutenant Blake?" One of the uniformed cops called out from the darkened parking lot. "You better see this."

Blake, Bobby and I jogged over to the blacktop covered in copper shell casings. The uniform sent a beam of white light down onto a face, pale and waxy. The dead man's coat was open, with another Uniform holding a wallet. In the beam of the flashlight, the cop flipped open the wallet. A brass star refracted the light from each of its five points. Bobby let out a low whistle. Blake took his hat off and ran spread fingers through his coarse hair.

The badge was that of an Orange County Sheriff Deputy, one of Sheriff JJ's goons on the Jeffers and Coposey payroll. This dead peace officer was responsible for countless acts of extortion on local growers. The badge pinned on the wrong chest can turn an ordinary man into a tyrant, but using it to make a hit on a private citizen was beyond anything any of us expected.

Blake spat. He did not bother to wipe the brown dribble from his chin when he turned to Bobby, "Not a word, Gomez." Blake did not need to make threats; Bobby was a good guy and an even better reporter. He knew the story was not over and had to wait until all the details were in before he would go to print.

The uniform on one knee went on to tell us that he knew Deputy Marshal Dunkin. He had sat next to him recently at the *law enforcement pancake breakfast* at the fire station downtown. He went on with details of the day and things he had discussed with Marshal. I did not want to hear any of it. This man, peppered with lead, was

[127]

nothing more than a target for me - a target that shot first. I had to make that dead sheriff's deputy black and white; he was nothing more than a failed assassin. The dead man before me was not the badge - he was all the evil he committed from behind that badge. I could see the color drain from Blake's round face. He had had enough, but it was his job to hear it all, not mine. I walked off.

Bobby offered me a lift back to the hotel since my International was part of a crime scene and in need of major repairs. We tooled up Orange Avenue and swung into the Orange Court. We sat with the car idling. It was a long night and Bobby was not ready for it to be over, running his jaw the whole way.

"What do you think would make a guy turn on a sworn oath like that?" Bobby stared out over the wheel at the road ahead. I wanted out of the car and go upstairs to a warm bed with a pretty girl as soon as possible.

"I try not to think about it." My words were soft. I was not solemn about killing a cop tonight or killing a man. He chose to get in a car with other hoods and try and take my life. If he had succeeded, there would be no pondering on whom I was, there would be a beer and a wad of cash waiting for him.

"You'll have to teach me to do that." Bobby continued talking, but I had enough. I cut him off, saying good night and reached for the door handle. Just as I jerked back, the door sprung open on its own. My hand shot into my coat, gripping the forty-five. The pimply-faced bellman that had done well with my truck was standing, catching his breath. His eyes were wide and his face was full of importance.

"Mister." He coughed a little as the icy winter air mixed in his lungs. Another voice shouted from the doorway of the hotel. Running out with both hands in the air was Jon, the desk manager. Leather soles slapped the concrete all the way to the car.

I got out of the car. "What is it?"

"Mister," Jon jumbled a few confused words. I grabbed him by the shoulders and shook. Then he spit out, "They took her."

My eyes widened and dried quickly in the cold night air. My limbs stiffened and my feet tingled. I could not speak for what seemed like minutes, but was just a second or two. The wind began to pick up, rustling the few leaves clinging to thin branches. A passing train blew a whistle. My brain, that was always a step ahead, fell silent. I could only react.

CHAPTER
9

"WHO?" I questioned uselessly. I knew who and why and where. The shock was slowing me down. It is always about women. The last time I was like this, the dame in the passenger's seat wound up dead. Her blonde hair, caked with dried crimson goop, fanned out on the asphalt. Not again, I told myself.

Jon described the two men. One was extra large and the other short with an accent. The Coposey Syndicate had my girl. There was no reason for it other than to get to me. So they wanted me that bad. I still had sixty rounds in my Thompson and another twelve for my Colt. It would be enough to put these rabid dogs down. County Sheriff or not, I was gunning for them all.

Giving me a slap across the chops Bobby brought me back to the living. We stood in the cold staring at one another.

"Sorry pal, but you kinda needed that." Bobby rubbed his hands together taking out the sting. He was right, I was frozen, and not from the cold. The innocent woman who had already suffered the loss of her only brother was now in danger because I could not stop them. The woman who pulled me out of a whiskey bottle was now frightened and alone. The glow of a girl can light even the darkest life. Sonya had that glow and another woman in my life did too, once. Her light is gone now. It was shut off by greed, but not for money - but rather ownership of a person. Now Sonya's light is in danger of dimming because of greed of money. The perpetrators cannot hide behind the badge a second time.

I felt my face warm with blood. My left eye twitched. I said, "I needed that Bobby."

I had neglected Jon all together. His teeth began to chatter from frost and the nerves. I pushed his short frame towards the doors saying, "Go on back now." It made little sense, but all I was seeing was red, literally.

Lieutenant Blake's car rumbled into the horseshoe drive of the Orange Court. His one red light circulated along the top of his unmarked blue car. Blake pushed the door open. He stood half in the car, one leg planted on the concrete drive. The news was all over my face, he did not have to say a word. He said to follow him.

Sitting in the front seat of Bobby's car I watched the street lamps pass by. We were headed south on Orange. Anger was rising in my gut, pushing acid to the back of my throat. My hands began to vibrate. Thoughts of Raulo and Vinny with their hands on Sonya spun my mind into a zigzag. I had killed two of their men tonight, starting a craving for something only a bullet could end.

We pulled into the police station parking garage. By now my leg was bouncing and I was tapping my fingers along the knee cap. I told Bobby not to pull in there. This was Blake's way of saving his job. I had a job to do and it was outside the law. Twenty years and a gold watch would not be waiting for me if I colored inside the lines. My retirement was a life with Sonya, away from this fruit stand town. Bobby would not listen. He told me I needed to trust my friends on this one and going in alone would only get Sonya and I killed.

Bobby's car slid in next to Blake's. I jumped out and fogged up the glass on Blake's door before he could pull the handle.

"Damn it, I'm not doing this your way, Blake." Steam seeped from between my gritted teeth. I balled a fist and pounded down on the roof of the dark blue sedan. I spun swearing once more.

Blake got out. He lifted up his pants then picked out the chaw in his lip. "Shut up and come with me." His tone was singular, as was his expression. He looked at Bobby and cocked his head. I felt two hands apply pressure to my back and we moved as one to the stairs.

We went down one flight and crossed the station lobby. Headquarters had become alive. It was a living organism. Cops in and out of uniform hurried about, some coming in through the door half-asleep, others guzzling coffee to keep awake. The law was the organism and the police, the white cells fighting off an infection. This body was burning with a fever.

I anticipated a turn for the wide staircase leading up to homicide. Blake grumbled something and we moved to a long hallway. The hall muffled the sound of hard working cops. We stopped at a door marked boiler room and went through. Inside was a metal stairway with rigid steps that resembled large metal bicycle pedals, the kind with teeth that would split your shin if you slipped.

Descending the steel steps, Blake said over his shoulder, half-apologizing, "We don't know how far the Coposey reach is. So we need all the privacy we can get."

The basement was damp with a rotten smell. Everything had a film on it from the railing to the cement walls. The room was cramped with two large oil tanks and piping running in multiple locations. In the middle of what space was available was a small round table, the kind you find in a French café big enough for one cup of espresso. The ADA stood on the other side of it, his coat off and thumbs hitched behind suspenders. He had two days growth on his face and the once blond hair was a stained greasy ash. The man next to him was crisp and laundered. Everything about him was average. Middle priced suit, nice shoes, but worn, and a hair cut that required little maintenance.

"This is Agent Owens," Henderson could save the introduction; it was obvious Owens was FBI. "We are dealing with a federal case now."

I spat.

"Something wrong, Mr. Chamberlain?" Henderson's words carried a tired sarcasm. I opened my mouth, but he spoke first.

"I'm here to make the arrest, Mr. Cotton." Owens's expression did not change.

"Meaning what, exactly?"

Blake stepped in, "Cotton, this is still our case. It's just that this whole damn thing is so deep we need the feds to put whoever we drag out away for a good long time."

"Yeah, well, I would like to put them in the ground."

"If it comes to that." Owens cracked a faint smile. It was just enough to assure me he would not be taking over the investigation. "I also come bearing gifts of information. Our Miami branch has been building a case on the Coposey Syndicate for months. We know how they operate and their targets of interest." He pointed to an open file covering the small table.

Bobby, not wanting to waste the opportunity of reporting from the inside, flipped through the papers in the file. I said, "I get why they would come after Blake and I, but why snatch Sonya?"

Owens scratched at his smooth jaw. "The Coposey Syndicate cut their teeth on kidnapping. It's what they do. I suspect they are after more than what we have here." With an index finger, he referenced the file.

Rage blindness had clouded my mind since the hotel. Only now could reason penetrate through it enough to question: "Why her?" No one knew about the secret ledger, and even if it was about that, Sonya no longer had it. They sent a hit squad after me and Blake, so taking her would gain no advantage.

Blake went over to the phone on the wall. He mumbled something into the line and hung the receiver. Standing shoulder to shoulder around the table, he said, "Someone came in today that may be able to shed some light on this." We all looked around at one another in silence. There was no point in conjecture until this mystery guest arrived.

The door at the top of the stairs opened. Light from the hall cascaded down the darkened stairwell. Back lit, I could make out a uniformed cop. Pressed against his side was a man with a pair of cuffs holding his arms together. His form was tall and lean. The uniform marched him down the steps, carefully holding him by the bicep.

From the single lamp hanging above, I made out the wrinkled and worn face of a man in his seventies. His sparkling ring was gone, along with his watch, tie and handkerchief. His suit was wrinkled and looked to have been turned inside out before being put back on. All the details that separated a wealthy man from the rest of us were gone, making the old man just another number in the jail cell. Missing most of all was the glimmer in his eye that had been there the night he and his man Careep picked me up in front of the red head's place. That spark was his real wealth.

I growled, but kept from lunging after him. I knew he had become a puppet in all of this. Once the Syndicate had you by the balls, there was nothing left to do but suicide. That killing-of-self came in three ways: giving in to the mob, giving up to the authorities or a bullet through your brain. Clinton Jeffers decided it would be death by cop.

"Good evening gentlemen." Jeffers choked on his words.

I butted in, "Can it Jeffers! Get to the point before I beat it out of you." Jeffers's eyes peeled back, he looked to Blake and ADA Henderson. No protest came from the group. For the first time since being with Sonya, I felt relaxed. This mob business was out of hand and it centered around Jeffers' involvement. Playing it straight would waste time and the men around me knew it.

"Yes of course, Mr. Cotton. To the point of the matter, as you are all aware, members of the Coposey Syndicate have," he cleared his pipes once again, "taken over my depot." His eyes were tired and red. The mask of success

[135]

and arrogance was gone, beneath defeat and hopelessness. Jeffers was the image of a man who had lost.

"So what are you offering that we don't already know?" I grumbled.

"Raulo and Vinny, the men that paid you a visit, Cotton. They are the ones you want. I was foolish enough to think I could manage the Syndicate and keep it out of Orange County." Jeffers started to go on about his plan to make and launder money on the side through his car accident scheme, getting paid through Miami Trust. He could then turn around and use the reported accidents to intimidate the local growers who opposed higher depot fees. A heartfelt confession must do wonders on his old shriveled heart and would play out in court to win at least one juror's favorable opinion, but it meant nothing to me. I wanted Sonya back, alive and unhurt.

"Damn it, Jeffers!" I lost it and sprung the five feet between us. I grabbed the lapels of his wrinkled suit. "Where is she?" I demanded shaking the old man. His face went white and he pinched his eyes shut.

"I don't know." He shouted back. His knees went out but I held tight, keeping him eye level to me.

"You don't get off that easy. I will kill you Jeffers, even if I have to follow you to whatever hellish prison they send you to rot." I began to shake him. His numb legs flailed. He kept his eyes shut. Blake stepped in and pushed us apart, sending Jeffers into one of the boilers. His old bones reverberated off the metal tank and he crumpled to the floor.

From the floor the old man began to cry, "I'm sorry, I'm sorry. It's all my fault... When I found out the extent the Syndicate was willing to go to take over the county, I left. It cost Careep his life and now the Clementine girl."

I lunged at him once more screaming for him to shut up. This time both Blake and Henderson grabbed me.

With both his arms covering his wrinkled old face, he said through sniffles, "I don't know why they took the girl, I swear. They have my daughter as well." His body shook with labored sobbing. We left him there on the damp cement floor with his grief.

Willimina showed up once again in the middle of the action. She was there when Henry was killed, knocked out in my office by men looking for me and now she was locked up some place with Sonya. Locked up somewhere were the only two women in a year to show me affection without payment - all because of me. I began to feel like a heel, that in some way I was a bad omen to all women unlucky enough to meet me.

"This time we have overwhelming force behind us." Blake began to lay out his strategy. I might as well have tuned it out. My mind was burning up with fever. As Blake went on about state police joining us to circle the depot, I was lost somewhere in the words and actions of the past few days. Taking Willimina made little sense. If Raulo thought holding Willimina would keep Jeffers from turning himself in, the plan failed and she was dead. Jeffers turned himself in after the fact, knowing full well of Willimina's fate. The way he sat crying out for repentance, pleading to go back and do it all over again, came off as sincere. I wondered what he was repenting for.

Blood Oranges

"So we just wait them out. With that size of a force, they will have to come out sooner or later." Blake hovered over the little table with his fat finger pointing down on an aerial view of the depot. It was an old advertisement Jeffers had taken a couple years back, showing the size and volume of the new depot. The familiar oval logo was at the bottom. I stared blankly at the oversized photo. Blake asked me two times what I thought. I was silent.

"I like it, Lieutenant." ADA Henderson said with a grin.

"Cotton, I said Cotton, your thoughts?" Blake had a bulb in his lip causing him to lisp slightly.

"Yeah, great plan Lt." was all I said. I could feel everyone's eyes hone in on my lackadaisical answer. My skin got hot and sweat ran down my sides collecting at my waistband. "Where do we go from here?" I asked breaking the tension. The men gathered around me, expecting me to come up with a plan or find the holes in Blake's plan or just outright object. I decided to keep my mouth shut.

Blake went on with head counts and car placements. He rattled off a list of names of cops he knew he could trust and the ADA assured us the Staties had been handpicked. We broke and made our way out of the damp boiler room. Two by two, we went down the hall. Bobby let everyone know he had to piss and I felt a tug at my left cuff. Blake agreed we should get it all out now so we don't when the shooting starts.

Bobby and I ducked into the men's room with Bobby's hand tugging on my collar.

"What gives, Cotton?" Bobby's voice echoed off the green and white tile squares covering the bathroom. I leaned against the sink. "Spill it, will ya?" He persisted, wagging a finger too close to my face.

"Alright, newspaper man. Might as well let you in. I'll need your help anyway." I grinned and Bobby relaxed for a second, then realized helping me would require more gunplay.

"I'm going to have to shoot more bad guys, aren't I?" His swallow echoed off the tile.

The door to the men's room opened a crack, and ADA Henderson muttered to get a move on. Blake was ready in the other room with a plan for the siege on the depot. I held my finger to my lips and Bobby understood not to say a word.

The reporter and I stood in the back of crowd that had gathered around the plans drawn out for the siege. Everyone was taking it serious but me. I could care less. It was a joke and a waste of time, but they could not see that. They were so hell bent on doing it by the book and rounding up every one of these scumbags. You don't let a dog eat at the table, because it is a dog. You don't treat these grease balls with respect because they don't have any. They are nothing but cheats who would rather use thick skulls to scare decent folks rather then get a real job. Well I had something tucked under my coat that can crack those skulls and I was itching to use it.

While Blake was talking, I was formulating my own plan. When their planning was over, everyone nodded knowingly, letting Blake know they understood it. I fought back a smile when my turn came to nod. I knew what I had to do, but it was not laid out in that meeting.

Down in the parking garage, Blake handed me back my Thompson. He said he checked it out of evidence and I would have to return it to him when this was all over. I promised him I would. He offered me a ride to the depot, but I told him I would ride with Bobby. He climbed in his dark blue sedan without taking his eyes off me. There was some detective left in the veteran cop - it was a scent I did not know I was giving off. Blake ran his hand over the wheel and spit a string of brown juice to the concrete floor. He dropped the car in gear and pulled out.

CHAPTER
10

BOBBY and I sat in the car with it at idle. The heater blasted and I cupped my hands over one vent. My knee was bouncing again.

"You gonna let me in on what it is we're doing? If I miss the whole thing cause you got a feeling or some shit..." He let the threat drop as he backed the car out of the spot.

I said, "Can you get an address from the paper?"

"No sweat." In this cold snap neither of us would be sweating much, but there was a group of guys I wanted to make sweat. I knew where they would be, and it was not the depot.

We got to the newspaper and it was much easier getting past security when I had Bobby with me. The elevators were shut down for the evening, so we had to take three flights of stairs. The hall was dark with the only light pushing out from beneath the occasional office door. Beside each office door was a corkboard. Each board had different articles and papers pinned to it. The offices with lights on also hummed with sound. Behind one door was soft music, behind the next, a typewriter being beaten to pulp. We continued on to a door simply labeled *Roberto Gomez*.

I stopped just outside the door, "You have a directory in here or something?"

Bobby went into the dark office. He neglected to turn on a light. Like a blind man in his own home, he knew exactly which way to go in the darkness. "I have to get something first." He said rummaging through a desk drawer.

Bobby emerged with a candy bar in his hand and a smile on his face. "Bribery, my friend." I followed him back down the hall.

We went down one flight of stairs and came out onto a well-lit floor. It was an open space with rows of desks. Three of them were occupied. Along the right side and far wall were offices with dark wood-grain doors and a floor to ceiling pane of glass beside them. All of those offices were dark. Bobby snaked through the countless desks, making his way to a tightly woven blonde beehive. She looked up from punching her typewriter and let the chain around her neck catch her glasses.

"Roberto, what a surprise." Her accent was heavily local. She reached a bent wrist out, but did not commit enough to reach him.

Bobby smiled, "Hello Julia. I brought you something." He handed out the chocolate bar with an equal southern draw. She received it with both hands. Cupping it in one hand she laid the chocolate on her desk, keeping the hand over it.

"Presents will get you anything. Dinner will get you everything." The corners of her mouth went up and the lines around her pale blue eyes darkened. I cleared my throat and her cheeks turned purple. She let out a little coo and put her glasses back on.

"I'm sorry, Roberto, I did not know you had a guest present." Her hands ran over an already flattened skirt.

"Julia, this is Cotton. I need an address and wondered if you could get that for me."

"Sure thing, Mr. Gomez." The pair of them turned to me in unison.

"I need the location of Butterfield Groves, run by a man named Sam." I dropped my ass down on top of an unoccupied desk. Julia scribbled down the name and excused herself. She walked, pinned at the knees to a wall of filing cabinets. Bobby and I watched her go. He took a seat in her chair and spun in a circle.

"Is this your idea of an office romance?" I chuckled.

Bobby's smile dimmed. He shushed me and said, "Watch it, would ya?" His tone softened to a whisper, "We got a thing, kinda. She's a divorcé you know." He said it like I cared. Good for him, I guess. All I could think about was finding Sonya alive and well. The image of her smiling, innocent face pierced my chest and suddenly I wanted to run out of there shooting anyone that stood in my way.

On the way back from the cabinets, Julia had two pair of eyes on her. She promenaded herself to the edge of the desk. In her hand was a slip of paper. She fanned it, not knowing how close I was to biting off her hand just to get it. "West towards Clermont... It's out past that Citrus Tower." She said matter of fact.

"The Citrus Tower." Bobby said, to no one in particular, his mind visualizing the route we would take. I snatched the address with directions. I left the pair of them to say their good byes that consisted of nothing but eyelashes batting back and forth and stupid toothy grins. I got as far as the door and stood holding it open, before Bobby snatched his hat off the desk and hurried to catch up.

We pulled out and went north, then cut west onto route fifty. It was late and it was cold. The streets were barren, even the migratory hobos found a place to hide. Once we were west of Highway 441, the four-lane route narrowed to two lanes. The traffic lights stopped telling drivers what to do and merely gave suggestions, blinking yellow for caution. At every major intersection, Bobby slowed the car anticipating a turn.

"What's with this tower?" I asked, breaking the silence of the night's drive.

"I can't believe you haven't heard." Bobby peered over the wheel, out at the pitch-black road ahead. We had entered citrus country. Miles and miles of fruit producing trees lined up in perfect rows. In the daytime, if you went fast enough, it was like watching a flipbook as each row in the grove passed by. Bobby went on, "Clinton Jeffers was one of the largest donors to the project. It's the tallest building around."

I'm sure Jeffers had received plenty of accolades and cut all the ribbons on the tower. A landmark dedicated to the local industry that made him rich and he turns his back on the growers, squeezing any little profit out of them. The police had him now. The charges against him should be enough to keep him locked up until his cold heart gives out. I had a smile on my face thinking about Jeffers in striped pajamas.

"What's so funny?" Bobby asked, glancing over but keeping his eyes on the road.

"Nothing." I mumbled and my face went right back to the grimness it had been in.

We motored on for another few minutes before passing a large billboard with an artist's conception of the Citrus Tower. It showed a white building, tall and rectangular. The sky behind it was blue with white clouds. In the foreground, a few cars filled spaces out front. In the back and along the sides of the tower, green bulbs represented the never-ending orange groves. I wondered why the hell anyone would want to drive all this way to stare out over orange groves. I told Bobby we were getting close and to be on the lookout for Simon Road.

We made the left turn onto Simon and I told Bobby to cut the headlights. He kept his foot hovering over the break as we coasted in the dark down a dirt road. As the car dipped below ten miles per hour, he tapped the accelerator, sending us another fifty yards on fumes. It was not long before light leaked through the rows of trees and we came to a house surrounded by orange groves.

On either side of the pale blue two-story wood frame house was a pair of tractor trailers wrapped in metal mesh and filled high with oranges. With the freeze warning out, all the lower halves of the trees were bare of oranges. These were the first to be lost to frost. Ladders were left in the trees along with conveyor belts leading to the trailers, still holding little orange globes. The picking had been halted prematurely.

Bobby killed the engine and allowed the car to coast another fifty feet, letting the sandy drive stop us before he put it in park.

In the front of the house a dim porch light cast shadows a hundred feet in every direction. In the back, a flood light hung on a twenty-five foot pole. A sign out front let us know we were at the right place. Butterfield Groves was scribbled in black on a white background, with the picture of a ripe orange beneath it. Bobby and I sat in cold silence watching for movement in the house.

After what felt like an hour but was more like twenty minutes, a fellow in a tweed coat and porkpie hat came out for a smoke. He was heavy set and made the wooden boards on the porch squeak with every step.

"I recognize him from my visit to the depot the other day." I whispered over to Bobby. He nodded without taking his eyes off the bum.

Once the thug was back inside, I told Bobby I was going to circle around back and take a look.

As I slipped out of the car, Bobby said, "Try not to get my car shot to pieces. I'm still making payments." With only a grin, I promised him nothing.

Hunched over, I crept around back, clinging to shadows as I went. Out there was a large grassy yard with a shed, backed up to groves. An upstairs window was illuminated. Black shapes moved against the drawn white shade. I scurried from tree to tree until I got to the shed. It was unlocked. I pulled my pistol and slipped inside. It was pitch black. I drew my lighter and struck it against my leg. A tractor, yard tools and a stack of boxes filled the space. I twisted off the gas cap and sniffed. It was gasoline, and not diesel. The hamster began to trot on the wheel. Next, I tore a flap off one of the cardboard boxes. I dipped it into the tank and was about to touch it off then changed my mind.

Back around front it was too dark to tell if Bobby could see me from the car. I hoped he was watching as I low crawled to the porch. There, I gathered some twigs and a few dry leaves. I laid them over the gasoline soaked cardboard. I was lying flat on my belly in the sandy soil ready to light off the cardboard, when the front door opened with a creak. I froze, with my chin in the dirt. My neck could not bend back far enough to look up to tell if my sprawled legs were in plain view of whoever was on the porch. To make matter worse, I had laid my pistol down to pull the lighter. I was caught cold.

From my position in the dirt, I heard the shoes shuffle away from me to the other side of the porch. A match struck as the thug sucked in tobacco. The match was tossed and landed a foot away from my makeshift campfire. A steady single stream of smoke rose from the glowing red match stem. My rate of breath increased and I sucked in the smoke from the match. The shoes pushed down on the porch some more as the thug meandered about. After the cigarette was done, he flicked it into the yard and went back inside. As the door opened and closed, I could hear a radio going and a few more male voices.

I peeled back a layer of the cardboard and lit it, making a short fuse. I scurried back to the car, where I met Bobby with the window rolled down and sweat dribbling down each temple.

[147]

"Shit, Cotton. That was close." He exhaled.

"No time to gab, Bobby. I lit a fire under 'em. As they come out, we'll disarm them. I want you to march them back towards the car. Any sudden moves out of them and let 'em have it." I turned back to the house in time to see the gas soaked cardboard ignite. The twigs and leaves smoked heavily in the cool damp air.

I ran up alongside the house. Bobby took to the other side. The flames barley licked at the windowsill before the door burst open and two hired guns came out. Neither man had on a coat, but both had pistols out. They waved them about scanning the darkest reaches of the yard, blinded by the light of the porch.

Bobby let out a whistle to draw them his way. I stepped out behind them and, in a harsh whisper, told them to drop it. I did not think they would comply until Bobby pulled back the hammer on his thirty-eight. They were caught in a soon-to-be crossfire and conceded to my terms.

From the shadows, I stuck my gun in the light and waved them off the porch. Their hands came up at the elbows, but hung loose. Bobby grabbed one by the collar and dragged him into the darkness with the other close behind.

Smoke plumed up. The door was left open a few inches and I could trace white smoke drawing into the house. A moment later, another thug came out hollering. It was Vinny and he stopped at the edge of the steps. His jaw clamored shut as he scanned the empty yard. He skipped the middle step, running to put out the fire as it began to spread. While stomping it out, I put the cold steel barrel of my forty-five against the bare skin of his neck. He became motionless.

"Don't turn around." I whispered. He grunted something and spun on his heels. I thumbed the hammer back as he reached inside his coat.

The forty-five caliber round went through his forehead just above his right eye. As he fell, his face held a puzzled look. His large frame crumpled in the dry leaves.

Black leaves with glowing red tips whipped up in the night air. The fire began to spread along the base of the porch. The front door snapped shut and soon after, a volley of bullets shattered both front windows. I covered my head as I felt glass rain down around me.

I looked up to see a figure run from the car and cut across the lawn. A few more shots came from both windows and the man went down tumbling end over end, carried by his forward momentum.

I went slack jawed for a moment, but kept my cool. It was hard to see through the smoke and night if that was Bobby or not. Either way, I still had at least two on the inside to deal with. I kept quiet, hoping whoever was inside would think I came alone and they had just gunned me down. Meanwhile, I fanned the flames sending the fire to the base of the porch. The wooden lattice along the base began to burn.

The door to the house cracked. A single eye peered out. It hovered at mid-door and darted back and forth. I leveled my pistol, but through the smoke I could not get a clear shot. The eye centered on me. A high screech pierced my ears as the door slammed shut.

The little weasels left inside put a woman up to the door as a look out. My hot breath steamed the night air as I exhaled. Before I could give thanks for not taking that shot, an arm holding a pistol barked from the window furthest away. I stood my ground and fired two shots. A grunt followed by another scream that carried over the crackling of the flaming porch.

Blood was now in the water and I wanted to taste it bad. With the front of the house on fire, the only thing left for the occupants would be to run out the back. I hurried around to the back door. As I came around the corner, I saw a muzzle flash and heard the buck shot tear through the sky. I ditched, face first, into the sandy soil.

I came up spitting sand, but all in one piece. Pushing back on the heels of my hands, I backed up against the clapboard siding. I grabbed half of a broken concrete block and tossed it through the window above. The block crashed through the window pane. Moments later another shotgun blast took out the remaining glass from the frame.

I did a stupid thing and jumped up to get a seconds worth of the interior of the house. I managed to see a red glow from the front living room as the porch became entirely engulfed in flames. In the dining room was Raulo, holding a shotgun in one hand and Sonya in the other. I could not make out anyone else. I knew there was still one other goon with a gun somewhere in there and had no clue whether or not Willimina was inside. I jumped a second time. This time Raulo was ready and fired the shotgun my way. The side of my face was blasted with splinters as the window frame came apart around me.

[150]

"Come and get me, Cotton!" Raulo taunted, in an insane voice.

"Let the girl go, Raulo!" I shouted over the building fire.

"I don't think so, Dick. You got a choice. It's me or her. Whatta ya say, Copper?" He fired the shotgun my way once more, just for effect. The Remington pump only held six rounds and that was the third. I would have liked to banter with him some more to get another couple shots off, but out of the smoky haze came Bobby.

He ran up with his palms open which was wise on his part. I almost shot him. He coughed and spat then said, "I got the one tied up."

"So that wasn't you gunned down back there?" I said with a smirk. When things got really tough and looked grim, for whatever reason, calm descended over me and I could deal with it. It was what has kept me in this game through all the bounties and hair raising antics of being a P.I.

"Damn it, Cotton." Bobby looked sore. Not everyone could keep calm in these types of situations. I hoped Sonya was one that could.

By then, the front of the house was too engulfed by flames to be a viable exit or entrance. They would have to come out through the back door. I was running the risk that Raulo and the goon with him were not the down-with-the-ship types and would eventually give up or trade Sonya for a chance to run. It would only be a chance because once I had my girl back, I was going after them with hot lead.

I sent Bobby around to the other side of the house to guard the windows and make sure they did not try to climb out.

A few more shots busted out the remaining windows in the downstairs. The smoke inside the house was getting too thick. I had to get to Sonya now, or risk her dying in a fire I set.

The run across the light-flooded back lawn to the shed attracted attention and bullets. I ran in a zigzag until I crashed through the shed door. Inside, I fired up the tractor. I let the motor warm up for a moment while I figured out how to lift the scoop on the front end. Once it was up just below my eye level, I hit the gas and busted out of the shed. The door slapped back, busting off its hinge. I mashed the accelerator down hard as bullets and buckshot sparked and ricocheted off the metal tractor. My head stayed low, peering up every couple of seconds to make sure I was headed straight for the back door as I raised the scoop higher.

Raulo yelled from the rear window what I took to be obscenities in Spanish as the tractor plowed into the house. I jerked forward, almost going over the steering wheel.

Bullets pinged and sparked around me as I climbed up the scoop and onto the roof of the house. I ran for the window and dove through. Crashing through the glass, I toppled over a dresser. I was on my feet in a hurry as steps crept up the wooden stairs, just outside the bedroom.

The door kicked in and the goon waved his pistol around. Too bad for him it was the wrong room. I pulled the door back and fired two quick rounds into his back.

He sprawled forward with his arms out, landing smack on his face. I put in a fresh clip before heading for the stairs.

With each step down, the air grew thicker. I could hear coughing from the dining room below. Suddenly I began to sweat. The calm cool that I had outside faded quickly when I saw a glimpse of the back of Sonya's chestnut covered head. My throat was dry and I tried to swallow, but nothing went down.

Raulo had one arm around her neck and a pistol out in the other. He was making wide sweeping motions, turning fifteen degrees after each one. The pair was locked in a static two-step. He knew I was coming, but did not know from where.

In the distance, a siren belched. The fire had been spotted. Raulo had no idea if it was the police or the fire department or both. He grew more careless with each sweeping motion.

"Give her up, Raulo." I shouted down.

He fired off a wild shot toward the stairs. "You've killed her Cotton, you've killed us all."

I could hear the crazy in his voice and knew what he was planning. A lifelong criminal like him would never just give up and be arrested. He also would never allow himself to be in a fair fight. I was not going to get the one on one with him I so badly wanted.

I took another step. As it creaked, Raulo fired. This time the bullet whizzed by me, impacting the plaster over my left shoulder. I jumped the remainder of the stairs taking a hard fall on the wood floor and rolled behind an overstuffed sofa. Bullets ripped through the fabric, blowing stuffing into the air. Sonya cried out.

I put my face to the floor and looked across the room from under the couch. Two pair of feet tangled up and moved side to side in a dance neither wanted to be a part of. I tried to line up the barrel on one of Raulo's legs, but the smoke was making my eyes fill with tears. A clear shot was impossible for us both.

"Cotton," Sonya cried out through the thick black smoke, "Do what you have to, just don't let him kill us both." Raulo covered over her mouth as she mumbled something else. I couldn't make it out, but did not have to. It was enough to get me on my feet.

I fired off a shot wide to let Raulo know I was going to kill him even if it meant Sonya died. He tried to return fire, but the good girl from Indiana put up too much of a fight. She bit down on his arm and kicked wildly with her leg. I marched forward, slowly at first. The Cuban tried to level his pistol. He squeezed prematurely and fired into the wooden floor. He swore again in Spanish and shoved Sonya to the ground.

I began to charge with all my might as Raulo's nickel-plated pistol steadied in his hand. His eyes grew large as he thumbed the hammer and straightened his arm out toward Sonya. Sonya covered her face and screamed into her hands. I felt the flames nipping at my back as a horrible squealing sounded just outside. The porch began to collapse, bringing down the front of the house. Hot red embers blasted through thick black smoke, sucking out all the remaining oxygen, ripping the cry from my mouth.

I collided with Raulo. We crashed over the dining room table and onto the floor. Laying on the floor, gasping for breath, I looked to see Sonya on her hands and knees. The hem of her dress was pulled up over her nose and mouth. Tears rolled down her cheeks, collecting soot as they evaporated from the sheer heat in the burning house. My throat was dry as a desert and my eyes burned. My jacket was covered in tiny red dots that quickly turned black, a few embers sinking through to my skin. Raulo crawled for the gun he dropped in the tackle. I grabbed a hold of his ankle. He kicked out but I refused to let go. The heel of his shoe connected with my jaw rattling my teeth, bringing back the pain in my skull from the sap he used on me two nights ago. Still, I hung on.

Sonya coughed and wheezed. She went face down into the smoke. If I didn't get her out now, she would die. Anger grew inside of me, turning me wild, and then I saw another face. It was that of a blond I had known years earlier. She was lying in the street, blood coming from her ears and mouth. She, too, was coughing and clinging to life. It was Fiona, my ex-partner's fiancée. She called out to me for help, but I was trapped, pinned behind the steering wheel.

"Cotton," she said. I heard my name again. Fiona never called me Cotton; I was always Chamberlain to her.

I rubbed the soot from my eyes as Sonya came into focus. She lay on her side looking into my eyes. She smiled a little girl's smile letting me know she would be okay now and was no longer in pain. I had seen that expression before.

Whatever miniscule amount of oxygen left in my lungs was enough to push my muscles into action. I reached up with my other hand and drove a fist into Raulo's crotch. He rolled onto his back, bringing his knees into his chest.

I crawled on top of him and let fly two crushing blows. His body went limp. I got to my knees and staggered over to Sonya. Grabbing her, I dragged us both to the kitchen. Busting out a window I called for Bobby to move the tractor. He was already on it, steering it back. The rear doorway opened up as oxygen starved flames sucked towards us. With all I had left, I carried Sonya out of the smoky inferno…

***

I woke up on my side with an oxygen mask over my mouth and nose. I was laid out on a stretcher, being wheeled into the back of an ambulance. The sun was rising in the east, punching a yellow hole in the black, winter night sky. Doctor Keenan and another man with a stethoscope were hovered over another stretcher a few yards away. I ripped the mask away from my face to call out. Instead, I began a coughing fit that ended in black tar dribbling out of my mouth. A man in a white coat gently laid me back to my side. I tried to resist but felt the sudden urge to relax and let that deep black calm water wash over me as it had the night I was sapped.

CHAPTER
11

THE hospital room was small. One side of my bed was a foot from the wall and two feet from the other wall. I wondered if this meant I was doing better and that was why I was now in what used to be a broom closet. I was still on my side. A band around my waste with a strap out to the bed rail held me there while I slept. I once saw the same getup with a bounty who was shot in the ass while fleeing. My back must be in pretty bad shape for them to leave me chained up like this.

To the left of the bed was an end table with a buzzer mounted on it. I reached out with my right arm, stretching stiff muscles to reach it. I pushed down on the little red button and held it a good five seconds.

It did not take long for a nurse dressed in all white from her shoes to her paper hat to come through the door. She had her hair pulled back tight. Her red lips really contrasted with the rest of her pasty white appearance.

"Mr. Cotton, you're awake." She wore a smile that went with the uniform.

"Good observation, nurse." I said, though the only sounds I made were that of two sheets of sand paper grating together.

"You must take it slow, Mr. Cotton. Please, for the sake of those burned up vocal cords, try not to speak. Doctor Hull will be in shortly." She stepped to my side and held my wrist to take my pulse. Updates were scribbled down on a clip board, and then she peeled back my eyelids to watch my eyes. I guess they were normal looking because she scribbled something else down and left the room.

A minute later, the doctor came in. Doctor Hull was tall with slicked back black hair and draped in a white coat. His eyebrows arched in sharp points, like two little hairy right angles above each eye.

"Welcome back to the land of the living, Mr. Cotton." He said dryly, curling the corners of his mouth. I bet he said it to all his patients. He peeled back my eyes once more, just as the nurse had and looked in. When he was satisfied I scanned the room for a mirror, fearing my face had melted in the fire the way both of them took interest in my eyes. Next, he came around behind me and poked at my bandages. I cringed a little here and there where he prodded my wounds.

"How's Sonya?" I managed to painfully scrape coherent words through my windpipe.

The doctor retracted his hand from my back. He stood silently behind me for a moment then came around so I could see his drawn face. My heart was thumping in my chest, drumming its way right out of my throat. I mumbled something more, but it was inaudible.

The doctor stood looking down at me with his arched eyebrows dancing above his eyes. He left me there in eternity while he chose his words.

The doctor smiled once more, changing the entire downward design of his face and said, "She suffered a little smoke inhalation, but otherwise is just fine. And you will be too, if you care to. Now get some rest." He turned to the nurse. "Nurse Stein, when you feel Mr. Cotton is ready, he may have visitors." He looked back at me and winked. It must have been all over my face. I was hopelessly in love with that girl from Indiana.

There was no window in my broom closet, or clock from which to tell time. Fading in and out of consciousness, I could not track days either. After a while, I began to stay awake longer than I slept. Nurse Stein came in on a regular schedule to check on me and, on one visit she brought solid food, well Jell-O, anyway. She propped me upright to eat. My tongue was swollen thick with a nasty film covering it; I swallowed whole little bites just to avoid chewing on the edges of my tongue. It went down smooth enough.

There was a faint tapping, almost a scratching at the door. Nurse Stein poked her head out. From behind I could see her dark curls bob then she fully opened the door.

Soft amber eyes with a crick above in the brow and chestnut curls hiding away in a lavender hat emerged from the doorframe. My brain was signaling my face to contort into a smile but I have no idea if the message was getting there. I do know the fear smoothed from her face as it eased into a big toothy grin.

Sonya's feet did not touch the ground as she crossed the floor to my bed. Nurse Stein was quick to warn her not to hug me tight, but I was ready for it. She swung her arms around me. Her lips gently grazed my cheek settling firm on my jaw. She pulled back and looked me in the eyes. The little fold between her brows showed again.

"Is it that bad?" I tried a smile, separating a hundred healing breaks in my lips.

"No. No worse for wear, Cotton." She hugged me tighter.

The thousand points of pain emanating from my back as my love squeezed me tight, quickly faded with a deep-sinking cavern in my chest that filled up with fear. I had spent any number of days lying on my side, strapped to a hospital bed, so as not to move and I never once asked for a mirror.

I swallowed sand once more and said, "Well, you still look like a million bucks, kid." I forced a smile and the splinters returned.

Sonya let out a little chirp of a laugh and said, "Honestly, Cotton, it's not that bad. I spoke to Doctor Hull and he said you should be out of here in a couple more days."

It was nice of the good doctor to inform her first of my condition. She was smiling and pecking kisses on both of my cheeks. I allowed it to continue a few rounds, then with my free arm held her at a distance.

"What about the case, what about Jeffers and the Coposey Syndicate?" I asked.

She sat on the side of my bed and folded her hands in her lap. "Lieutenant Blake has kept a tight lip about it all."

I laid my head back on the pillow. Normally I would be craving a cigarette right now, but the thought of purposely inhaling smoke seemed ludicrous. These last few days, the doctor's drugs kept me coming in and out of consciousness. My mind was able to fixate on very little.

All that came through were flashes and heard sounds of the adventurous few days leading up to me being in a hospital bed. Now that I was weaning off the drugs, the cloud that blotted my thoughts was gone and clear images were now in the forefront. Anger was back. My finger began to tap on my thigh.

Sonya looked down at her shoes. She took a breath and said, "I guess I'm just not enough for you right now." Her focus centered on a hang nail, picking at it to avoid eye contact.

I wanted to hold her in both arms and tell she was wrong, but I could not. Not only was one arm tied to my side, but also because I knew she was right. Henry Clementine came to me with suspicions that turned out to be true. A crooked man was getting away with crimes against the very people that put him in a position of power. Clinton Jeffers over-extended himself by inviting the Coposey Syndicate to lend muscle and now it nearly drowned him.

"I need you to call Blake and get him down here to fill me in." I reached out and touched the side of her arm.

Sonya continued to stare at her hands. "Sure, Cotton." She said.

"Hey, listen to me. Once I know this is all over, we can go anywhere you want. But I need to finish this, for your brother."

She looked up at me with big saucer eyes that were covered in glass. A single tear rolled down over her rosy cheek. She grabbed my hand and held it to her cheek saying, "Oh Cotton, we will. We'll get so far from this lousy town and keep away from oranges as long as we live. Even if we die of scurvy, I will never eat another orange."

"Let's not go to extremes." Leaning forward I planted a kiss on her lips. I pulled away and continued, "Now go get me some clothes so we can get out of this nut house."

Sonya jumped up and made for the door, stopping to give me a smile before heading through. Nurse Stein came back over and flipped through my chart.

"Mr. Cotton, you are not cleared to leave." Her tone was sharp with authority.

I chuckled, "Lady I can't take another day in this closet."

She went on to lecture me on the dangers of leaving against medical advice and how doctor Hull would not sign off and it could jeopardize any further treatments of my burns. I leaned back and shut my eyes. Images of Sonya's pleasant smile and ruby red lips filled my mind. I was holding off conclusions about the case and instead focused on what Indiana looked like this time of year. I mentally inventoried my own thin wardrobe and decided I would need a new coat.

Sonya came through the door, just as the phone next to my bed rang. I smiled to my girl as I answered the phone. "Yep."

"Chamberlain Cotton's room please." I recognized the voice as Blake's; he however did not recognize mine.

"This is Cotton, Blake."

"Shit, Cotton, you sound terrible! But I guess it's better than dead." He was swearing already, whatever news he had could not be good. He went on to fill me in on all the happenings the staff at the hospital did not.

Raulo, Vinny and two more of their thugs were dead thanks to me. Jeffers had made bail during all the chaos and went back to the depot.

Sonya heard Blake's gobble through the phone and she dropped her smile as my face contorted with anger.

Blake went on to say, after taking down Sheriff James they went back for evidence and found Jeffers sitting in his overstuffed leather chair, a single bullet hole in his temple. Suicide is such a cowardly thing to do and it takes away all the fun out of the furious vengeance I had planned.

Hearing Jeffers was dead, the rest Blake had to say carried little water. My back was peppered with hot embers from the fire and I nearly lost my vocal cords, not to mention the constant hacking up black tar from my singed lungs. It was not as bad as the doctor made out and I am always a quick healer. I let the good lieutenant continue until he was out of gas.

Blake paused to take a breath and I jumped in, letting him know he had it all tied up and I needed to get some rest.

"Okay Cotton," Blake said through the line. "Get yourself better and I'll take your statement on the grove shootout later."

"You got it Blake, though, it could be awhile." I hung up. Sonya was standing near me with a frown. "What's with the frown, kid?" I asked, sitting up.

"I thought you were doing better, but you just told Blake…" She mumbled something at the end I couldn't make out.

[163]

I swung my feet down on the cold linoleum and smiled at her. "Get me in some trousers and let's get the hell out of here."

Sonya lost the frown and tossed me a pair of grey wool slacks. It took some doing, but I managed to get the pants on with one arm. To put on a shirt, I had to remove the bandages holding my left arm to my side. My shoulder was stiff as I raised it to get into the shirt, but otherwise felt okay, nothing broken. Lastly, Sonya draped an overcoat across my shoulders. I asked about my hat, but it turned out to be a victim of the fire.

"I really liked that hat." I said as we walked down the hall of the hospital.

"Don't worry, I'll get you another one. It's the least a girl can do for saving her life." Sonya squeezed my hand tight. I squeezed back.

"I think you got that backwards, kid."

"Oh and Cotton," she said, laying her head on my shoulder as we continued through the hospital.

"Yeah?"

"Merry Christmas."

CHAPTER
12

THE next five days passed just as they had in the hospital, except I was not alone in the bed and we were in the Orange Court with room service instead of hospital food. We ordered champagne, steak, lobster, anything and everything we could. For five days, we never left each other's side, not even to shower.

On the morning of the 31st a call came in. I was on my back, finally able to enjoy a cigarette again. Sonya sat reading a magazine at the small dinette.

"Hello."

"Mr. Cotton?" I recognized the voice.

"Willimina, how nice to hear from you." I was not sure what to say to her. Her father had just committed suicide over this whole mess, not to mention Sonya and I nearly died. With all the aftermath and recouping in the hotel catching up with Sonya, I had completely forgot about Willimina. I felt terrible, not having thought to ask Blake about her.

"Yes, well with all that has been happening, I wasn't sure if it was alright to phone you and Sonya." Her voice was soft, without the resentment it held when I turned down her advances. "In an effort to repair the damage done by father, I am hosting a new year's party tonight at the house."

"That is a great idea Willimina. By house, do you mean…" Again, I was not sure how to handle this conversation. We had never spoken pleasantly to one another; our conversation topics generally contained the subjects of murder and extortion.

"Yes, that one. I do hope you and Sonya will attend."

"Sure, we'll be there."

"See you around eight then." There was childish excitement in her tone. I repeated it and hung up. Sonya was already on the bed next to me with an ear near the receiver. There was no need to tell her what Willimina wanted. Sonya jumped up and began sifting through the mess of clothes scattered about the hotel room floor.

"I have nothing to wear." She said, with her hands running through those chestnut locks.

I slipped my arm around her waist. "I prefer you that way." I said, then pulled her in.

***

Clinton Jeffers's home was right out of *The Great Gatsby*, if it was set on the Mediterranean. It sat back on a lake in the town of Winter Park, just north of Orlando. A long gravel drive lined with one hundred fifty year old oaks guiding you back to a whitewashed façade, brown wood trim and terra cotta roof tiles. All the lights were on inside, bathing the shrubs lining the circular drive in yellow light. There was only one big black sedan parked out front and no valet insight.

Sonya sat next to me in the cab, fussing with the hem on her blue dress. She had not packed anything formal for her trip to the Sunshine state. The trip's purpose was to claim the body of her brother and get his affairs in order to

[166]

leave Florida and never come back. While getting ready for this shin-dig, we discussed our plans for the future. Sonya made it very clear that she was over the sunshine and the oranges. I was beginning to agree with her. I could live up north - all I would need was a new coat.

"Well, where is everybody?" Sonya said, finally looking up from her hem. The cab swung around and we got out. I handed the cabbie a fin and told him to keep the motor running for a little while, and then split if we did not return. He nodded and threw the car into park. I took Sonya's hand as we ascended the three large burnt orange tile steps. I grabbed the heavy knocker and let it drop against the large single wooden door. At the center of the door was a small iron hash mark, behind it a pane of glass. I saw movement.

The door opened. Dixon stood holding the knob. His black suit looked fresh and pressed. Mustard yellow outlined his left eye where it had once been deep purple. His eyes pinched and he swallowed as if bile had risen in his throat. I could not help but smile.

"This way." He said flatly, waving a hand to usher us in.

We followed him in, remaining hand in hand. The house was just as grand inside as it was out. The thick clay tile continued on through the entry way. A stair case semi-circled up along the wall to the left, leading to an upstairs. The walls held fake Sixteenth Century Spanish antiques, highlighting the nation's conquests of the Americas. An iron chandelier hung from the domed ceiling. It must have held a thousand points of light, and all of them blazing, forcing me to squint as I removed my hat. Dixon took it as he led us to the room beyond.

Sonya and I walked slowly. Each step echoed off all the tile and plaster. Willimina must have got the invitations in the mail on time. The house was bare. Each room we passed was empty, void of the expected laughter, music and storytelling most parties hold.

Sonya's nails dug deep into the back of my hand just as the hair on the back of my neck began to stand. She was onto something with her suspicions. Either we were extremely early or this was a party for three. The house was empty with the exception of the four of us.

We came to the one dark room in the house. Light from the hall laid out a yellow rectangle on the eggshell colored carpet. At the very end of the rectangle was a pair of pointed toe heels, with cramped feet inside them. Blackness draped over the rest of the still figure.

"Come in." A soft voice from the dark called. Willimina struck a match and held it near her face to light a smoke. The flame flickered and reflected off her wide mocha eyes, setting them off into a mocha fire. She whipped her hand and the match went out, leaving only the orange glow of the cigarette.

Sonya reached out her free hand to hold my arm. I wanted to reassure her everything would be okay, that I had dealt with psychos before. I *had* dealt with psychos before and it never ended well. I had to think quick and clear. Coming off a few days doped up in a hospital bed left me in a fog that I had to shake right away.

We stood in the doorway until I felt hard steel press against the middle of my back. Somewhere deep down,

Dixon was psychic because the barrel twisted right in one of the burns still healing on my back. My shoulders tensed and I fought the urge to swing an elbow backwards.

Dixon ran his free hand under my arms and around my ankles. I fought off another urge to raise my knee and crush his face. Instead, I kept my gaze on the end of that cigarette dancing in the dark. I followed it around the room, going to my left then to the right. I assumed she was standing behind a desk or a couch now. When Dixon was done with his pat-down, he shoved me further into the room and slammed the door shut, leaving us with only the glow of tobacco to talk to.

"Okay Willimina, what's the gag?" I asked letting my body relax a little with the hope it would ease both girls' moods.

"To the point, Chamberlain." She said my name slowly, letting it linger. "I will call you Chamberlain. Cotton seems so childish."

I could feel a tremble crawl up my arm as Sonya's knees began to knock. I squeezed her hand and released it. I stepped in front of her. The past two weeks had been long ones and I was a day away from leaving this shit-eating town behind. All that was left was this crazy bitch and her driver.

Willimina dragged long on the cigarette. I could make out her face. Her eyes were fixed on me. She was just out of reach. I waited for the exhale to take another step towards her.

"The hero stands, guarding the girl he loves. How cute."

[169]

"What's this all about?" I inched forward. I suppressed my breathing. I felt Sonya's finger tips at my back. I did not want her to be here with death waiting in the air. Willimina was sure to make some kind of play on her.

"Tell me Sonya, did Chamberlain tell of our affair?"

Sonya sucked air deep, cutting me right across the gut. I wanted to look back at her, but kept on the orange glow.

"Cotton…" Sonya's voice was light. I reached a hand back and managed to touch her side. I pinched softly then patted her, pushing her back from me slowly.

"Yes. It was just last week that we shared a moment of passion in his office, the two of us and a bottle of bourbon." She laughed aloud filling the darkness with her sickness. "You see girl, when you are as mature a woman as me, you learn the hidden secrets of men. You know what they know and what they want. And, most importantly, you learn how to use it to get what you want." The orange glow dropped from her lips and smashed into an ashtray. The squeal of wood on wood covered the distance between us. Soon another match flared. It was held waist high in one hand and in the other a small thirty-two automatic.

"You've closed the gap between us, Chamberlain. That is a risky move, but then, you are a real hero." The match burned and was dropped in the ashtray. "Yes, you have yourself quite a man."

In the crazy minutes we had since entering the dark room, I had not given much thought to Willimina or the role she played in all of this. She was always an afterthought to me, throughout this investigation. From the time we met in the street, there was not much to take notice of. Suddenly, here in the dark, it all came to light and Willimina was in the dead center of the whole thing.

"You're nuts lady!" it might as well have been fire coming from Sonya's mouth.

"What's the matter little girl, they run out of big strong men up in Hicksville?" Willimina moved while she spoke. "I just want the same thing you do, a strong man to wrap his leathery hands around me at night." I could tell she was still moving about the room, but the plush carpet silenced any steps. That worked for the both of us.

I sensed her moving to my right. I fought all the urges to swing left to right and reach out at whatever was before me. The worst thing I could do would be to move my feet. There was a chance I could end up twisted around and lunge for Sonya instead of the crazy dame with the gun.

Willimina brought me here as a test of strength to fulfill her twisted view of what a real man was. Well, I did not plan to disappoint.

I said a prayer and leapt. When I was a kid and swam in a pool with my friends, it was a great game to see who could swim the length of the pool under water with one breath. On days the water was too chlorinated, you could not open your eyes or else suffer the rest of the day with them burning. So you paddled with one arm while the other is outstretched waiting for that concrete wall. Here I was, back in the pool, holding my breath and reaching out in the blackness.

My hip caught the side of the desk, spinning me to the right. I could feel silk brush the back of my knuckles as I fanned out my hand. A shrill laugh filled my ears followed by the pop of the thirty-two. Then it was Sonya's turn to scream. I continued my momentum into a bookcase. My shoulder crashed into the shelf as my neck bounced my head into books. I swept my arm along the shelf sending books out into the darkness. Another shot.

I jumped for the muzzle flash. This time, I got both my hands around that silk. I jerked it towards me running my hands down the sides. She let out a sickly giggle of pleasure then squirmed, ending in a mousey cry. My palm cupped the hot steal. Resisting the habit of flinching, I clenched down, singeing my hand. With my left, I hooked shoulder high. I connected with a ball of curly hair. I swung again and the weight of her body thudded on the plush carpet. I dropped with it, holding the hot steal. The gun fell freely into my hand now. I slipped it into my pocket.

Both hands swept the padded carpet. I was on hands and knees now, feeling for a body. There was none. I stood up and felt around the room.

"Sonya, don't move." I said giving away my position. My foot kicked the desk. My hands ran along the surface looking for a lamp. I found a chain and yanked.

The light flashed on, blinding me for a moment. Once my eyes adjusted, I found I was facing a pair of windows in what looked to be a study. I spun around.

"She has the prettiest little features, don't you think Chamberlain?" Her voice snaked. Willimina had a hold of Sonya. She held a small blade to Sonya's upper left cheek. The blade was too small to threaten anyone's life, but if it were dragged along Sonya's face, there would be a constant reminder of my failure. I had to separate the two.

"What am I supposed to do now, Willimina?"

"Save her of course. You are the hero here, aren't you?" She let out that sick little giggle. "Don't you coward out now. No, I wouldn't like that. She wouldn't like that." Her voice went high, with one hand, she pulled back on Sonya's dark hair, pressing the blade against her skin with the other. "Tell me about the fire, Chamberlain, about how you saved this girl's life and mine too, if I had been there."

"I thought you were there. I thought I was coming for you both."

"And who would you have saved first?" She shifted her weight between her feet. I tried not to look at Sonya. I needed to keep eye contact with Willimina.

"Why do all of this?" I asked, waving my hands. "Why trap us here? If you wanted a rescue, you should have set it up so Dixon out there was hurting you. Then I could have swept in and took him down." I was getting her attention. Her eyes broke with mine for the first time since the light came on. She was thinking it through, seeing where she could have set all that up. Willimina was craving a rescue. She wanted tough men. That is why she went with Tom first. Things were getting hard on the growers at the depot and Tom stepped up. When he wasn't strong enough, she finagled her way in with the Coposey boys. Once I took them out, she could not resist. I was beginning to think her father's death may not have been suicide.

Willimina began to latch onto my idea. Her attention was waning. I locked eyes with Sonya and twitched my blue orbs at the door. She nodded slowly, letting me know she would go on my signal. I did not wait long.

The distance between us was about six feet. Somehow, I covered it in the blink of an eye. Sonya ducked and rolled out of the way. I tackled Willimina to the floor. I struggled to get a hold of her knife-wielding hand. She bit and scratched like a cat in a bag. Hissing and squirming beneath me, I struggled to hold on. Sonya disappeared from my peripheral view. I did not want to kill this woman in front of Sonya, but I did not think she would leave me the option.

I circled my hands around her neck. The veins at her temples turned a dark purple as they rose to the surface of her pale skin. Her cheeks filled, flushing red as my grip tightened. I could hear Sonya behind me, repressing a yell as she looked on in terror. Still my grip tightened. Willimina beat at my sides with little balled fists, struggling one last time before the oxygen was finally cut off. Her eyes rolled back until they were all white and her body went limp. I held a few more seconds.

Sonya touched my shoulder and I eased up. I got to my feet and looked down on the spoiled rich girl who only wanted to be loved by a strong man. Then I remembered all the pain and death she had caused, and I wanted to finish the job I started.

"Is she…" Sonya could not finish the sentence.

"No, just unconscious." I wiped my sweating palms on the legs of my pants. I spotted a phone on the desk and I told Sonya to call the police. She grabbed the phone and spoke softly to the operator. Dixon was still in play on the other side of that door. I gave Sonya the pistol and told her she had to use it if Willimina woke up. She assured me she could, despite her hand shaking when she took the gun.

I went to the door and listened. It was quiet on the other side. I twisted the knob slowly and pulled the door into me a couple of inches. Not seeing Dixon, I slipped out. A couple of steps down the hall and I heard, "Hold it right there."

I turned around slowly to find the driver holding a pistol. I looked him dead in the eye and said, "You have a choice here. You could try to empty that gun before I get to you, or just hand it over."

Dixon's face went white. He swallowed hard as sweat bubbled on his brow. I thought he might call my bluff, instead he dropped the pistol on the tile floor and ran for the door. I went over and picked it up. There was no use chasing him.

I went back into the study. Sonya ran up to me and buried her head in my shoulder. I cupped the back of her head and held her there while she sobbed.

***

Lieutenant Blake arrived minutes after the first patrol car rolled in. Willimina was coming to, just in time to get slapped with cuffs. She hollered about her father calling the mayor on her behalf. The patrol man shook his head with pity; she was unaware her father was dead.

I told my story to Blake, who listened again to Sonya describe everything. The stories lined up and there was nothing left for him to do but ask if we wanted to press charges. I declined.

"Just see that Willimina gets help." I said, to which Blake nodded. He asked me what I was going to do now.

"Blake, all I want to do is get the hell out of this orange stand town. I'm heading north." I shook his hand. He shook mine and wished me good luck.

The End.

Bonus Story:

Chamberlain Cotton sat at the bar getting drunk. It was a futile exercise, the alcohol never made it to his brain. He had not worked in some time. Today, as he had with the last twenty, started with a beer. Three pours later he was on to brown liquors. The barkeep at South End Bar advised against the order of drink, but Cotton did not care. In the last three months he could not get drunk enough to feel hangover remorse for the night before.

Hours earlier a low hanging fall sun found a break in the drapes, hitting Cotton in the face. He rolled out of bed. After a quick fried egg there was nothing else to do for the day.

Indian summer removed his jacket, setting him up at the bar in a worn out Cleveland Indians tee shirt and jeans frayed at all ends. He didn't bother with a button up or a tie today or the last hundred days. Today, Burt the barkeep had a reason for Cotton to get dressed and back to work.

"You know Sandra Cross?" Burt muttered the question as he poured a shot for Cotton's beer.

Cotton stared into his pint glass.

"Well, do you know her or-"

"Yeah, yeah Burt what about her?" Cotton kept his eyes buried in golden ale.

"She was found beat to a pulp yesterday. Some mug roughed her up good." Burt bent and came up with a crate of clean pint glasses and moved to the other end of the bar near the door. A decent looking man and woman came in the bar; decent people do not drink here. He stood tall and lean; she fit tucked under his armpit. The couple looked around for recognizable faces. There were none.

"Do you serve food?" He asked.

"Nuts."

"Excuse me." The lean guy replied.

"Nuts." Burt pointed at a bowl then another saying, "Pretzels."

The couple shared blank faces. Burt walked back down to where Cotton was sitting.

"Should I know this gal?" Cotton swallowed the last of the ale.

"I mention it because the pair of ya is always chattin' it up til close most nights." Burt ducked behind the bar.

Cotton sifted through blurred images piecing together random thoughts trying to tell a story. The fog began to lift. He saw legs pinned at the knees. A hand on his arm with nails chewed to nubs and lips plump and ruby red. A shotgun blast of freckles below each green eye circled in thick liner held long lashes. Her deep black curls bounced as she tilted her head back in laughter.

"Sandra." Cotton said to an empty bar.

Burt stood up with a cup of steaming joe. He put it on the bar in front of Cotton. "Land lady found her outback of the building next to the dumpsters. Sandra hasn't said a word..."Burt kept talking but Cotton could not hear him.

Cotton passed on the coffee. He pushed off the bar laid a C note down.

"What's with all the bread?" Burt did not let the questions keep him from snatching up the cash.

"Back taxes." Cotton made for the door without looking back.

Water sputtered and spit out of the head eventually gaining a steady stream. Cotton did not bother to check the temperature. He made it quick. There was no curtain to keep the water off the tile floor.

Toweling off in his one room dump Cotton looked around at the stacks of dishes scattered about and a bed with no sheets. He had been to Sandra's apartment a few times. Just to keep drinking after the bar closed. She was a cute girl for sure but Cotton just wanted more whiskey. There was a couch with a blanket and throw pillows. The kitchen was in another room next to the bedroom. Once things got hot and heavy between them, Cotton got as far as the bed. He face planted into down pillows that smelled of citrus, and then passed out. He woke up on the couch wrapped in the blanket.

Sandra had already left for work. She was a secretary by day and hustled her head shot around agencies at night. The nights she got call backs she wound up at South End. The nights she got a gig she wound up at

[179]

Blood Oranges

South End, in time for last call after being at the higher class places celebrating. Those were the nights Sandra was most fun.

Cotton's studio apartment smelled like stale piss and a gas leak. In the top dresser drawer he would find the bounty hunter badge and a gun, instead he decided to put on a tie.

Tucked under an oak and covered in dried leaves sat Cotton's Willys Jeep CJ. It was flat black with white wagon wheels. Rust bubbled under the paint along the usual rear welds in the tub. The aftermarket hard top was still on from last winter. The arctic fronts where pushing south again so the hard top was best left on. The front bumper and the passenger side rocker panel were both crumpled in.

He worked the key back and forth; it had been three months since he parked the Jeep. The battery had to be dead so getting the door open was least of his problems. He sat looking at the passenger seat. He needed a drink. Sandra worked her pretty face into Cotton's mind pushing out the ghost in the passenger seat.

The battery was dead. Cotton pushed the Jeep to the edge of the drive, gave it one more push and jumped in. Popping the clutch the 258 fired. The tail pipe popped and he revved the motor to get it warmed.

The little Jeep fit easily between a pair of sedans parked along Jackson Street. Cotton made his way up to the seventh floor. His head was empty of thought as routine led him back to Sandra's apartment. Up the stairs and down the hall there were no images, no assumptions, and no ideas. Cotton knocked.

Jasmine came to the door. Her black hair had streaks of white-blond, the color was always changing. This was the closest thing to natural Cotton had seen.

She kept the door close to her face, "She's asleep Cotton."

"I just need to see her." His breath was heavy with malt and hops.

"Not right now. Come back tomorrow maybe." Jasmine tried to close the door.

Cotton's foot was quick to fill the gap. Jasmine swore in her native Cuban, but caught herself as the volume rose. She sucked air between her teeth and let the door fall open.

The apartment was a mess. The coffee table was covered in glasses with food encrusted plates balancing one atop the other with discarded food wrappers on top of that. It did not resemble the citrusy scented well situated apartment Cotton remembered.

The bedroom door was ajar. It pushed in easily for Cotton who stood filling the frame. He had seen people beaten, did some beating himself. There were days he shot thugs and thugs shot him. Those men were ugly before their beatings and would remain ugly after. Sandra was not one of these. She had a smile that could melt a heart or cool a temper. It was good to have a girl like that around South End or any other dive.

The part time model and full time secretary was lying still on her back, face up and wrapped in bandages, she was poised even while unconscious. Had Cotton not known that blood filled bruises swelled beneath the gauze, he would guess Sandra was rehearsing the part of a sick woman on a daytime soap.

He stood over her, not wanting to wake her, but needing to talk.

"Sandra." Cotton touched her arm.

The only reply was a raspy labored breath.

Cotton touched her arm saying, "Sandra I need you to wake up. I need you to tell me who did this." Then his hand touched hers.

A slight moan proceeded her saying, "Cotton, is that you?" One eye was covered. The blood shot eye searched left towards the man's voice.

"It's me sweat heart. I won't take much of your time, you need your rest. Just tell me, babe, who caused you this trouble." Cotton knelt beside the bed.

"It was terrible. He came outta tha-"

"Don't recount it babe, just tell me who. Did you get a look at his face?" Cotton kept his words cold.

"Yeah. Billy Stanton." Sandra closed her one good eye. Cotton watched a tear roll out of the corner and get absorbed into the white cotton wrapped around her face.

Things started to heat up inside Cotton, things that had been doused in enough alcohol to drown an elephant. As the fire welled inside, he began to feel trapped there in the model's room. He needed to get

[182]

out, get his body moving to level off the pressure of his racing heart. He needed to feel Billy Stanton's flesh break apart under the force of his knuckles. He needed revenge.

The Jeep fired on command and even chirped a little as Cotton gunned out onto the street. This time his head was not empty of thought. With one consuming focus, he pushed the Jeep to its mechanical limits. Vengeance, retribution, hate, all of these feelings culminated into images of the worst physical harm a man could do to another. Memories of all the bones he had broken, lips he had busted and skulls he had cracked on the job pushed the limits of his mind. Cotton's brain filled with pressure, his eyes ready to explode with white-hot radiation. The hate fueled bad things.

The gutter-splashed sky finally opened up. There was no time to stop and put the doors on the Jeep. Cotton pulled a poncho off the passenger seat and slipped it over himself during a red light. The radio was on but he wasn't listening. It was another few blocks to Billy's studio. William Stanton was a photographer. A few years back he made it big when some bedroom photos of an otherwise plane Jane turned out to be the local senator's daughter. Suddenly, being shot by Billy Stanton in your underwear was a high class. Class, there is a word without definition. Women who wouldn't take it off for their husbands were now topless on a bearskin rug smile for Billy and his camera.

Blood Oranges

Billy did not know what do with his success and like most folks pissed it away on booze and self-importance. When one of the "tasteful" boudoirs photos made their way into a smut rag, a few angry husbands made their stand on Billy's face. The shining star faded and so did the level of clientele. No one would touch him. He survived by sending a few saved negatives to X rated magazines in Japan. Sandra used him because he was local and cheap.

Cotton parked the Jeep a block down from the studio. Sitting, staring out the windshield, a few scenarios flashed through his mind. One version had Billy holding a knife, another with Billy going into a rage so Cotton puts him down like a rabid dog. The last thought was less fun but more real, Billy crumpling to the floor pleading for his life. A few gut punches would suffice then.

The poncho was off as the rain turned to a heavy mist. In the quick walk to the studio, Cotton rolled around in his mind why he wanted to beat Billy so bad. Sandra was a pal, just a good time girl. There was no love or real relationship, nor were there thoughts of one. Still you don't beat a girl, so that is why all the hate would rain down on Billy's head. A final memory, the one he had spent months drowning in emerged as images of deep purple blotches with yellow edges spotted flawless porcelain skin finished off with a lump protruding just beyond a blonde hairline. Baby blue eyes pink from crying looked up at Cotton. It wasn't Sandra he was fighting for and it wasn't Billy he wanted to kill.

The memory stopped Cotton cold. The dent in the Jeep fender and rocker panel was part of that memory. He had picked her up a few blocks from where he stood now all those months ago. On a rainy day like this, but colder, inside the Jeep was warm. The doors were on that time, Cotton was prepared. Victoria stood with a hand covering half her face, the half Luke Wilmington beat in. He would be back any minute and if he caught her getting a ride from Cotton, it would end in gunfire.

Her call came in while Cotton sat at his desk in the bail bonds office. Years ago he and Luke went into business after they bailed out Cotton's cousin. The brother tried to skip and when Cotton and Luke caught him they found their calling. It was good for Cotton because he had quickly been following in his cousin's no-good steps. The chance to carry a gun was all Luke needed to be in on the business.

Cotton said hello but heard only deep sobbing on the other line. This was not too out of the ordinary considering the line of work. He told the lady to calm down and start talking if she wanted his help. When the sobbing stopped, Cotton knew exactly who it was and why she was calling.

Luke had been on a downward spiral for several months. When offered dope as a payment he really went into the deep. Cotton wanted to dissolve the business and pull up stakes but there was too much cash tied up. He had to be careful of how he went about it. Victoria was just one more cog in the machine of problems for Cotton.

Victoria Stanton was thin with curves and bends forcing a second and third look. It was too tempting to keep your focus on one spot for too long, and when she began to add motion to the curves, all concentration was broken. Luke met her out at a bar on Main, where bars strung together like laundry on the line. Soon she started coming around more and more. Cotton couldn't angle her attraction to Luke. He was good enough looking with wavy black hair and hands that could palm a basketball. His smile pronounced his jaw and calmed his eyes, melting most gals' hearts.

Inside the Jeep, Victoria kept her left hand over her face. She said only "drive" and did not look back, but kept her eyes to the floorboards. Cotton glanced over now and then as they rode along. He looked at the diamond on her finger and wondered when things changed. Finally, at a traffic light she dropped the hand. Her face was red with undertones of wine. A honk from the car behind broke Cotton's stare.

"I won't let him keep on with this." Cotton pushed the Jeep into second. A rage was beginning to cloud his mind. Dots of everything wrong Luke had done suddenly connected in Cotton's head. Missing cash, bonds that were way to high, payments in dope, all of it part of Luke's shady dealings and now this.

"I'm sorry Cotton, I had no one else to call." Her words gurgled from deep in her chest.

"We'll go back to my place and we can sort this all out." Cotton was only thinking of crushing in Luke's skull. Victoria curled into a little tight ball. She wanted to make herself disappear. No matter what Cotton did this was going to end badly.

The rain picked up and the little wipers moved as fast as they could. Water in the gutters backed up turning streets into canals. The large tires of the Jeep waded easily through the rising tide. Cotton turned off the boulevard making for his place. Luke's Edsel headed up the other direction. The next turn was his street. Cotton got there first. As they turned left, Victoria was exposed in the passenger seat window to a gaping mouth Luke.

The Edsel's motor raced bringing the car alongside the Jeep. Luke's window went down and he began to shout. It was the usual slang for Victoria; tramp, skank, whore, but soon the name-calling went Cotton's way. Luke was shouting things like double crosser and back stabber. Cotton had been warned last time he stepped up for Victoria after the first time she caught the back of Luke's hand. For the most part Cotton backed off, after the first smack it was her own fault for what followed if she stayed. He offered one time to help her leave but she refused. That was supposed to be a one-time offer but in the last few months leading up to this car chase, Luke had progressively worsened. Drugs do things; make you act out in ways you never would sober. Right now Luke was looking to act out with murder.

Cotton saw the dry cleaners and his studio up above, but he couldn't stop. It didn't help that it was a Saturday and the street was packed with shoppers. There was nowhere to stop the Jeep. Looking back, he should have just pulled over.

Rounding the corner, Cotton dropped the Jeep into second and accelerated hard out of the turn. The tires spun on the wet asphalt. Luke's old Edsil could not handle the turn, he continued straight. Any safe place he thought to take Victoria, Luke would know about. There had to be some neutral ground they could go and sort out this mess.

Cotton cut up Malvern Street headed east. Victoria began asking where they were going and then sobbed repeating Luke's name. She was a mess, as strung out as her pursuer. He wanted her out and regretted ever picking her up. At one stop sign, she tried to bail out, exclaiming she could fix everything with Luke. Cotton grabbed her arm and held her back from jumping from the Jeep. Crossing Boulevard, the old Edsil ran up on the Cj 5, the grille crumpling as it impacted against the Jeep's mounted spare tire. Victoria screamed. She looked back between the seats at Luke and held out a hand as though Cotton was now a kidnapper.

Frustration was giving way to anger for Cotton. He slowed to make a right, which is when Luke leaned out the window and fired a couple of shots. That cemented it for Cotton; there would be no stopping to talk things out.

"Hang on, this will all be over soon." Cotton's cold steel words pinned Victoria to her seat. The Jeep revved. Distance increased as the Edsil was slow to get into second. Cotton watched the Ford disappear in the side mirror.

Screeching tires and a high-pitched scream from Victoria whipped Cotton's head to his right. A red MG, with a scared middle-aged man behind the wheel, slid under the Jeep. The CJ5 lifted into the air. The rear tire caught the left fender of the MG, bucking the Jeep like a deranged bull. Cotton shut his eyes. When they opened, Victoria was in the street thirty feet from the Jeep. She was a cream-colored lump with red wine pouring out from multiple spouts.

Luke pulled his car to a stop. He jumped out screaming. It was obvious to everyone standing there she was dead. A lifeless body has a look of absence. She had that look.

Cotton blinked a couple times to clear away the memory. The last time Cotton waited to interfere with a woman-beater it ended in the only death he regretted being responsible for. This time Cotton had designs to end it early while the girl was still alive. He crossed the street and headed down the block to the Stanton studio.

The mist subsided just before a heavy rain began. The drops falling large and round crashed down onto Cotton's scalp and shoulders. A steady current ran through strands of hair down his neck absorbing into his undershirt.

The heavy sliding door to the studio was unlocked and went back easy. A small waiting area was empty. Cotton pressed on to the heart of the studio, where so many housewives bared all for this creep, a place for showing flesh only meant for their husbands end up shown to the world. This slime ball was going to pay today, not just for what he did to Sandra but for the trust he broke of those other woman.

The room was large. One wall was exposed brick, one painted a baby blue. The third wall held three large windows. It was a nice space for sure, if it wasn't tainted by the smut and deception that took place among these four walls.

Half the room consisted of cameras, photos and rolls of film spread out over a large table. To the left, several backdrops hung creating different scenes. A few lights and a tripod stood just in front. Across the room was a bed, unmade, a sink and mini fridge. How convenient, a bed in the studio. Cotton wondered how many young girls with stars in their eyes were convinced it would be a good career move if they posed on that bed.

Sitting on a stool next to the table fooling with a flash was Billy Stanton. He looked up catching eyes with Cotton just as the flash went off. For a split second the pair was blind. As focus returned to expanding pupils, Cotton was one step closer to Billy. The photographer was familiar with the look on Cotton's face, it told him to jump up and defend himself. Billy decided in the moment of fight or flight to sore out of there like and scared crow.

He backed up cawing, raising his open palms as he backed down. Cotton kept coming.

"Sandra says hello." Cotton decked the photographer sending him spinning into a studio light. Hovering over the white backdrop of the set, blood dribbled to the floor from the corner of Billy's mouth.

"What'd, what'd ya do that for?" Billy stayed low to the ground avoiding eye contact with his attacker.

Cotton, without words, swung his right leg sending a size eleven shoe across Billy's covered face. The knotted laces burned as they scraped the underside of Billy's arm covering his face. The impact sent the frail perv back and over crashing to the concrete floor.

"You like to take advantage of women don't you, you weak little man." Cotton watched the dazed man struggle to get to his feet. "If you think those fooled husbands gave you a pounding, brother your perception of pain will change."

"What'd I do to Sandy? I told her those new headshots would be done by the end of the week." Billy slinked away as if he was the Hunchback. "You got this all wrong. Was that you threatening me this week, over that, that girl?"

Cotton ignored Billy's defense, "Go on a bender so bad you don't remember beating a girl to an inch of her life." Cotton kicked again sending his foot into Billy's gut, doubling the man over.

Billy gagged then spit. The long stream of dark pink drool touched the ground before breaking. He looked up.

"I never touched her, I swear. Listen pal you don't want to mess with me like this."

"Where'd you do it Billy?" Cotton pointed to the backdrops, "There? Maybe over by the bed when she refused to lay down with you."

"It was never like that with us I swear. She was here the other night and I snapped a few shots of her new hairdo. That's it man. I told you on the phone I wasn't messing around with anyone's old lady." Billy was backing away. He slid across the room to the metal frame of the bed and hoisted himself up.

The way he runs his life, Cotton thought, Billy must have multiple threats against him weekly, an entire line of fellows who want to do what Cotton was doing right now. He paced around the studio.

"You put her in the hospital Billy." Cotton took off his drenched sport coat.

"No way man. She left here just fine, happy even with the shots." He inched along the bed, staying between the bed and the sink.

"For once in your life man-up to something." Cotton moved to the end of the bed. Billy was stuck. He could try to jump the bed to escape but knew he could not cover that distance in time. He backed into a nightstand. This was the end of the line.

Cotton moved in. Billy dropped his hand behind him and reached into the drawer. He pulled out a .32 automatic.

***

"Here let me help you with that." Luke Wilmington sat beside Sandra's bed. He reached over and together they began peeling back the bandages from her head.

"It will be a relief to get this bandage off my eye so I can see straight. You know you really scared the hell out of Billy with those phone calls. He was so convinced somebody was coming for him, he went out and bought a gun." She sat up and peeled off the medical tape around the bandage.

"I had fun doing it. You think he'll know it wasn't Cotton?"

"Nah," She laughed, "Cotton will kill him first."

"Or the other way around."

Their heads tilted back in laughter.

***

Billy stopped only to grab a camera before running out of the studio. Cotton lay flat in an ever-expanding pool of warm crimson. Rainwater still in his hair worked into little drops running along the sides of his scalp as he stared up at the exposed rafters. He should have stayed drunk today, getting sober over some girl seemed so backwards.

www.ingramcontent.com/pod-product-compliance
Lightning Source LLC
Chambersburg PA
CBHW020245150626
46552CB00020B/242